STAR PRINCESS

Encounter in the Dark

Moses Solomon

In honor of
The Ursuline Sisters of St. Mary's School
Moscow, Idaho
For an Education That Has Lasted a Lifetime

My sincere thanks go to my editor, Suzy Vitello, for all her guidance in my first young adult work; to Dana Henderson, for his inspiring artwork; and to my wife, for her great ideas, and all her love and support.

Contents

About the Author

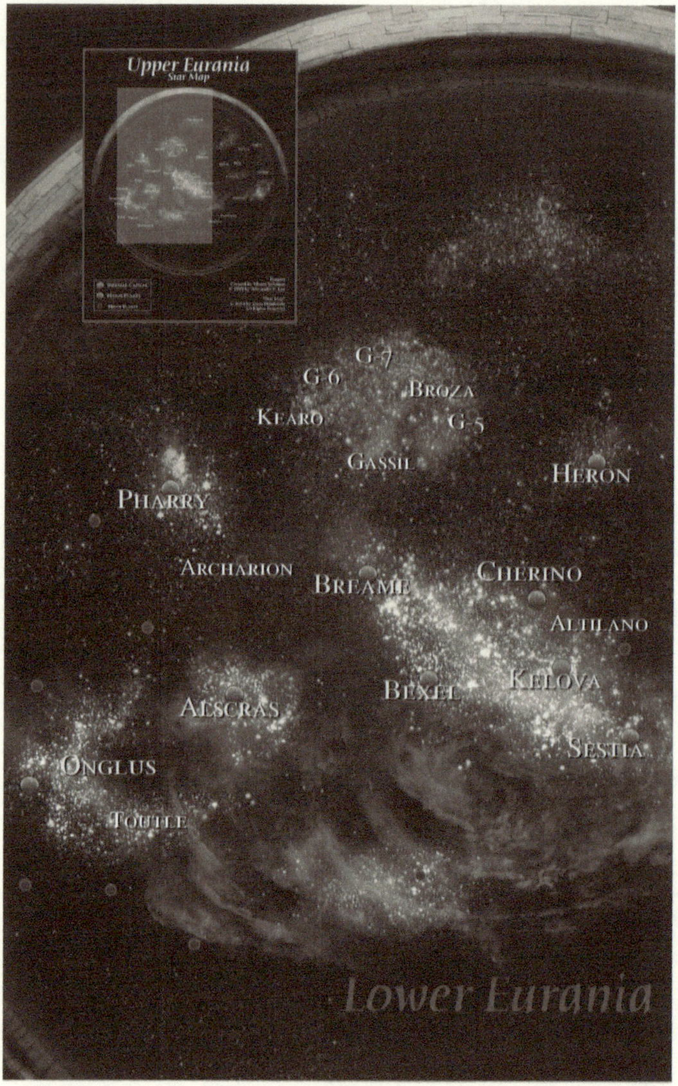

Upper Eurania
Star Map
G-7
G-6
BROZA
KEARO
G-5
GASSIL
HERON
PHARRY
ARCHARION
CHERINO
BREAME
ALTILANO
KELOVA
BEXEL
ALSCRAS
SESTIA
ONGLUS
TOUTLE
Lower Eurania

Prelude

Sixteen year-old Thericia, Princess of Alscras, was losing her patience. Her attendants—a full dozen women, both young and old—were taking too long with her hair arrangement. The emerald-accented tiara, which she had not worn since her father's fiftieth birthday gala, wasn't fitting properly. It was enough to make her want to pop someone.

Princess Thericia ran to the mirror to check over herself. Her forest green and ivory gown draped down to the floor. Her delicate studded earrings sparkled. The jeweled bracelets hugged her ivory gloves. Her makeup was scant. She always had a battle with her entourage to keep it subtle. This time, she'd won. She lifted one foot, then the other, and examined her matching ivory heels.

"No, this way!" The older stylist scolded the two younger ones. The woman took hold of

Thericia's upswept arrangement, wound it around three times into a classical Alscrasian wave, and pinned it. "Like this."

Thericia stared in the mirror. She hated it. The spiral wave was far too overdone, almost like a DNA helix. "I want it simpler."

One of the two younger stylists pulled the pin and let Thericia's golden-red hair flow down gently over her shoulders while the other tied a simple peasant braid.

"No, no, no!" Thericia protested. That was too simple, lacking in regality and command presence. She couldn't be a peasant for this occasion. She growled at the stylists and slapped a hand away with a loud "whack." Three of the youngest attendants recoiled, startled by her ferocity. "I'll do it myself."

She hated being the one who was always late, but her brother didn't have such issues with elaborate hair, poofy dresses, or variable-height shoes. He only had a simple military uniform, and that the same one every time. Even her scepter was almost as heavy as his ceremonial *cuxioblade*. Thericia waved everyone away, took hold of her hair in one hand, and her tiara in the other. She did her own hair for her father's birthday, she would do it herself for this occasion. But there was no avoiding being the last one, again.

"Late as usual, I see." The feisty, diminutive

Chief of Staff, Franklen, pointed to the end of the line, next to her brother, with his porta-com stylus. "Here."

"I'm sorry." Thericia ran out of her bronze stretch sedan and dashed past the black-clad security guards, skillfully lifting the long skirt of her gown a couple inches to keep from tripping over her heels, her attendants racing to keep up. She took her place, quickly straightened her outfit with a deep relaxing sigh, accepted her scepter from her aide, and looked about. "Otias," she whispered, elbowing the Prince, "don't hunch!"

The tall and lanky *laissez-faire* heir rolled his eyes and marginally straightened his back.

Thericia shook her head in disapproval. He always said she was an overkill on petty details and only humored her as his duty to his younger sister. She hated being patronized like a child. He spent hours each day alongside their father, learning the interstellar affairs of the empire. She didn't. Her role centered around protocol. Or propriety. She performed her public-appearance duties, not because she cared for them, but because they were...well, her duties. Glancing over at her attendants, she dismissed them with a nod to take their place with the rest of the staff along the wall of the terminal building.

An imposing military lander rested on the tarmac before her, billows of black noxious fumes rapidly dissipating into the afternoon breeze. Two stories tall and elevated on massive landing gear, it sported deep dark gray plating, two rows of glistening laser cannons on either side of the hull, and an oversized dual tail fin. As the ceremonially-attired Alscrasian royal guard, in shiny black with rich scarlet trim, stood at attention in single file before the titanic warcraft, the ramp lowered. Two columns of soldiers, the dusty gray-clad elite guard of the Gearmlian Confederation, marched out with charge-pak rifles slung over their shoulders and traditional *cuxioblades* hanging from their belts.

Thericia was sufficiently impressed. Unlike her father and brother, she never had opportunity to travel off-planet, except to nearby neighboring worlds under Alscrasian rule. Stifling a frown at the thought that she was a "Star Princess" in name only, she glanced down the family line, first at her brother, who stood at attention, then at her mother. Under her brightly jeweled tiara, regal Queen Jarina held a firm—almost stiff—smile across her face. Tense. Her father looked a bit more relaxed, but not much more.

Though her father, the king of Alscras, was officially the Emperor, she understood that any real power he held at the imperial level was the result of a hard-fought agreement by all the constituent dominions, especially the five core worlds, which included Alscras and the Gearmlian Confederation, the most-distant, most-talked-about member of the empire. Peace in the young empire had held steady for nearly fifty years with only an occasional minor incident on a remote asteroid or planetoid rattling the calm. And yet...the taut veins that jutted from Emperor Otias II's neck told Thericia his true feelings of the Gearmlian dignitaries who descended the ramp.

The imperial peace relied almost exclusively on the personal friendship between the King of Alscras and the *Primus* of the Confederation. It was something Thericia had overheard from her father only once, when he was confiding to her mother—and Thericia happened to be around the right corner at the right time. First, it had been her grandfather, King Otias I, and King Bhuthe of Breame. Now, it was her father and the Breamian successor, King Priot. As for the other major planets of the confederation, including the military industrial planet of Gassil and the resource-rich world of Kearo, support was razor thin.

The bright lights of the media blinded Thericia for a moment. It was a necessary irritant of being associated with the government. She had gotten used to it years ago, but it was still an annoyance that distracted her attention from the imposing monarch descending from the ship.

Gray-bearded King Priot wore a black and gold uniform of the old Gearmlian Corps over his square shoulders. An array of colorful medals decorated his chest and a gleaming silver *cuxioblade* hung from his hip. The Gearmlian *Primus* was taller and more muscular than Emperor Otias, a dominating figure who would make for a threatening personality but for a relaxed smile and a soft twinkle in his eyes.

Behind King Priot stood a young man who looked to be in his early twenties, wearing a deep scarlet and silver uniform of the Gearmlian revolutionary era, barely shorter than the King, with a square, clean-shaven jaw. A modest trio of medals lined his chest, and the brim of his hat lined neatly over his eyebrows. His steps were sharp and crisp, like those of an actual soldier.

Was that the King's son? She had never seen him before, though she knew that a prince did serve in the Gearmlian reserve in some unpublicized capacity. He didn't have a governmental position. As far as she knew, this summit was an arms limitation negotiation. What was he doing here? Sightseeing? Or did he have an unannounced military role in the proceedings?

Following the entourage of visiting soldiers down the ramp was the olive-skinned, shock-white-haired deputy *Primai*, with her bright red Brozan robes flowing behind her, accompanied by the bald-headed leader of the Gearmlian military in dark glasses, General Faut.

King Priot and his contingent lined up at the base of the ramp, in front of their military escort. A buffer of about two dozen feet separated the visiting delegation from the Emperor and his party—the Queen, Franklen, Admiral Kosolf, Prince Otias, and

Thericia—while the royal band played the anthems of Alscras and Gearml. Thericia found herself standing opposite the tall Prince. Of course.

When the music finished, the flashing lights began again as the visitors approached, flanked left and right by their guards.

After greeting the Emperor, the Queen, and Prince Otias, King Priot stepped over to face Thericia. She silently held her breath as the young Prince accompanied the King over and smiled at her. Without warning, her heart rapidly pounded with anticipation and her hands went ice cold.

She had never had this sort of reaction to anybody before, let alone a perfect stranger.

"Dear Princess," the King said with a rich low tone and a comforting smile, "I would like to introduce my son, Jomin, Prince of Breame."

Thericia smiled and held out her hand to shake with Prince Jomin. Gearmlians were customarily business-like in their greetings, or so Thericia thought. To her surprise, Jomin lifted her hand and gave it a gentle kiss on the backside. "A pleasure to meet you, Your Highness."

"And it's a pleasure to welcome you to Alscras," Thericia responded without missing a beat. "I hope your first visit will be an enjoyable one."

Jomin stepped aside, giving Thericia a moment to calm her adrenaline. King Priot brought the deputy *Primai* forward.

"May I introduce my deputy, Lady Ludzenia of

Broza."

The deputy *Primai* chilled Thericia to the bone. Her muscles tensed. Somehow, the smile, with blood-red lips narrowed and pitch-black eyes squinting, just felt untrustworthy. Thericia's mother mentioned to her—more than once—of Ludzenia, a humorless, mysterious figure who often stayed in the shadows.

It was just a feeling, the Queen had said, one woman's intuition of another.

Lady Ludzenia's appearance, though, unsettled Thericia. She had seen the deputy *Primai* on the imperial widecasts on a few occasions, and in person once before, leading a trade delegation to Alscras. But Ludzenia had never sported such an extreme appearance. Her usual gray-green short wave hairstyle had been replaced with the ghost-white static frizz, and her customary dark business suit with the blinding, fiery red robe. It was difficult for Thericia to unlock her eyes from Ludzenia's.

"Such a lovely young lady," the woman whispered more than spoke. "You were so much smaller, before." She gave her head a slight tilt. "Welcome back to your world?"

Thericia swallowed hard and took a deep breath to relax her fist before they shook hands. "Yes. It's a pleasure to see you again, Lady Ludzenia."

1. State Dinner

"Did you see him look at us?" one of the attendants gushed in a high-pitched voice.

"Did you see him smile at us?" a second added.

Thericia rolled her eyes. She knew that it was the Prince's duty to smile at everyone in public.

"I could have died." The first aide threw a hand over her forehead and playacted a swoon.

"I did die." The second crossed her arms over her heart and spun around.

Thericia cringed. She didn't know how much more of this she could take.

"How did his hand feel to you, Your Highness?" It was one of the middle-aged, matronly aides now. "No, how did his *lips* feel to you?"

Thericia shook off the question and stormed out of her private chamber, shutting the door on her laughing attendants and all the nonsense. While she could concede that it was technically not a handshake, it was still an official handshake, like any other greeting with a member of a visiting delegation. Even the exchange with Lady Ludzenia.

Girl talk, on the other hand, was killing her. None of her aides would be able to approach a Breamian prince. She did admit that he was somewhat attractive, clean-cut, slim but muscular, and decorated in a triumphant warrior's colors. But it was all celebrity ogling by hormone-driven young women. And older women, it seemed. Nothing more. Certainly, nothing for a roomful of working women to get so excited about. If anybody should be getting worked up about the visiting prince, it should be...well, her.

She sidestepped the small robot vacuum and quickly crossed the landing that overlooked the grand staircase at the foyer. After passing a series of rooms, she came before her parents' door and gave it a sharp rap.

Thericia hoped her father was in, and not huddling with Franklen or Admiral Kosolf, again. Meeting and greeting the Gearmlians was one thing, but state dinner duties and all the small talk were redundant and not real duties like issuing joint rulings or discussing trade strategy. She had only one question to pose him, and it was driving her crazy.

The door opened. Her father stood before her, fully dressed in a cream and gold jacket with pitch black braids on his sleeves, and his bushy hair meticulously combed for the media-covered event. She could see Franklen and Admiral Kosolf waiting inside the room.

"Thericia?"

Her father was busy. "I'm sorry." She felt bad for interrupting his meeting. "Do I have to...?" Before she could get the question out, she already knew what the answer would be.

"Yes, Thericia?"

Was it worth asking, anyway? Maybe she could still get a pass. "Do I really need to attend the state dinner?"

Her father sighed. "Thericia...."

"Nobody would notice my absence, father." If she was going to put the subject on the table, she may as well pour all of it out. "It's not like I'd have anything of political consequence to contribute to the dinner conversation." She dropped her gaze and her voice, but avoided hesitating. "Not like Otias."

"Thericia...."

Before he could speak further, she quickly added, "I could put the time to much better use. I've spoken to the instruction master about starting a course of self-study. Advanced history, philosophy and ancient religion, political science—"

Her father thrust his hand up, silencing her.

"Thericia, you hold a title. With the title comes responsibility. Each of us has our own individual duties. We've had this discussion before, have we not? Now please, everyone has much to prepare before tonight. And so do you."

Thericia lowered her head. Every time she brought up the subject, it became more frustrating. Two years ago, she would have been delighted to attend a state dinner, but it did not take long for her to realize that her "duties" amounted to doing her hair and her make-up.

But, the Emperor had spoken. After one last glance at her father's top advisors, Thericia decided, once again, to make the best of what she could.

With a deep breath, she obediently said, "Okay," and walked away.

Thericia gazed at herself in the mirror as she unwound her hair, releasing the cascading tumble of golden-red curls. It was a mess.

So was her life. Mastering her studies was one thing; playing the role of the Princess, though, was something else. With her brother, her father was all about business. But with her, it was all about the show. Just once, she would love to discuss the matters of government with her father, the Emperor.

She sighed. The state dinner would begin in a few short hours. More ceremonial clothing, more fussing about her hair and her face, more cameras. She could only hope the menu was interesting. The speeches, for sure, would not be.

After that, music and dancing. More gushing over by her attendants. Would some of them faint? Maybe, if they all passed out, she would be able to enjoy the evening in peace.

Thericia paused as the door clicked open.

Queen Jarina stepped in, two young female aides—one in pantsuit busy jotting notes on a porta-com, the other in an orange dress carrying a large case—in tow.

"How are we doing?" the Queen asked. She held Thericia's face up and gave her a quick exam. "Not quite ready, I see." The Queen released Thericia's face. "I know we need to review your staff." She pointed toward the two aides. "Would you like some help?"

The girl in the orange dress snapped open her case, revealing a multitiered make-up kit.

Thericia sighed. "Is my attendance absolutely necessary?" She wasn't hoping for an answer contrary to her father's. She just needed to talk it out with someone.

"I'm afraid so. It's an important occasion for the empire, and the media will be in attendance." The Queen's voice was stern, but she spoke with a smile. "Besides, wouldn't you like to get to know our visiting Prince?"

Thericia shrugged her shoulders. *Not really.*

"For all you know, he could be your future suitor. It would certainly be good for promoting peace in the empire."

Thericia jerked away. "Mother!"

The Queen laughed. "I'm joking, of course."

"No more boys!" She quickly bit her tongue, her

fists clenched, and stifled the urge to launch a tirade about ignorance and old-world convenient marriages with a long, deep breath. "I have more important things to think about," she said through gritted teeth, "like my studies."

"Of course."

"I'm doing just as well as Otias, don't you think?"

"Yes, Thericia. But we need someone to help entertain the Prince, tonight."

"Otias can do that—"

"He can't dance with the Prince." The Queen chuckled. "That's your job."

Dance? Thericia paused. Did Prince Jomin dance? If he did, would he ask her to dance?

"You like to dance, Thericia. You may enjoy it."

Yes, Thericia agreed, she and Otias had taken all the proper lessons in traditional and formal Alscrasian ballroom and of course, she showed more talent for music and movement than he did. Growing up, she always danced in her room to her favorite jazzy tunes, while he hid in his room and read in the peace and quiet of his ear plugs.

Perhaps it might be interesting to dance with a stranger, Thericia conceded. Would Prince Jomin know Alscrasian ballroom? Or would he ask her for an unfamiliar Gearmlian dance, instead? Maybe...

Thericia smiled at the thought that the night might actually bring her a new experience. Motioning for the two aides to follow, she headed for her closet to search for the evening's attire.

Thericia tried not to look too disappointed while she ate with Prince Jomin and her brother. The food was exquisite—fire-roasted *wafelbeest* steaks, carmelized roots, sliced marine delicacies, and wild greens—but the two princes conversed almost exclusively about their local sports teams. Except for *haissen* riding—which she was pretty good at—sports wasn't one of Thericia's many interests.

She gazed about the grand dining hall at the other dignitaries and listened to the orchestra, trying to ignore the crowd of lights and reporters lining the back walls. Emperor Otias and King Priot conversed together with Queen Jarina, Franklen, and Lady Ludzenia—who barely picked at her food —at their sides. Next to Prince Jomin, General Faut ate heartily in silence. Thericia didn't catch what her father said to King Priot, but everyone around the table suddenly broke out in laughter. King Priot gave the heartiest belly laugh of everyone. Everyone, Thericia noticed, except Lady Ludzenia, who only showed an icy-cool hint of a smile.

Thericia had long ago given up on trying to listen in on the adults' conversations at functions such as these. It seemed that they rarely spoke of state matters at social events. She found small talk and other inconsequential conversation suffocating, and this occasion had quickly devolved into the latest of a long line of uneventful, downright tedious, official meals. With Otias and Jomin engrossed in their debate on the various sailback racing strategies, the time passed slowly for Thericia.

Eventually, dessert was served. Triple berry cakes with Ruby Rose liqueur, one of her favorites. While Prince Jomin studied his pastry set with a cautious gaze, Otias supplied him the background factoids on the three native berries. Thericia could only wait politely for their guest to have the first bite. The rumination was agonizing—it was only a dessert, not diplomacy. This visiting prince was far too methodical for her taste. When he finally took a bite, she breathed a sigh of relief and dug into her own dessert.

"Let me show you my boundball team," Otias said to Jomin, pulling his mini-comp out of his back pocket. "I'm leading our palace pool."

Thericia grimaced. *Not the fantasy-league team again!*

Jomin chuckled. "I'm leading our pool, as well. We should have a match, during our stay."

Thericia sighed and ate quietly, barely tasting the sweetness of the dessert, her mind drifting away to thoughts of escaping the evening festivities to ride Torrence, her favorite *haissen*.

After everyone had finished, the staff cleared the tables as the orchestra played a nostalgic song from the traditional Alscrasian repertoire.

"I notice you still use a human wait staff," King

Priot said, eyeing the workers around them.

"For state functions, yes," Emperor Otias said.

King Priot leaned forward and lowered his voice. "We find robotic staff more efficient and less prone to errors."

Thericia's ears perked up, sensing a potential debate coming.

"Perhaps," the Emperor said with a smile, "but most of our visiting dignitaries appreciate the warmth and personal touch that only a living human being can offer."

Thericia smiled. The human way was the Alscrasian way. The Gearmlians?

"I am curious, Your Majesty." Lady Ludzenia paused to glance at King Priot. "If I may?"

"By all means."

Ludzenia folded her hands together. "We rarely hear of the non-human minority among your people. The indigenous Sonarians, or the Ethsokian insectoids, for example. What role do they play in Alscrasian society?"

"A valued, integral part," the Emperor said. "They are the primary growers of our agricultural bounty, the backbone of our transportation network, the main body of our service industries."

Ludzenia seemed to scowl. "Service industries, indeed."

Thericia stiffened at the woman's tone of voice. Her father had intended no slight against the non-humans, but Ludzenia clearly did.

"What role do non-humans play in Gearmlian society?" Queen Jarina asked Ludzenia with a terse voice.

The deputy *Primai* eyed King Priot, who nodded, before answering. "A very similar role, Your Majesty. 'Service industries.'" She spoke the phrase with a sly mock. "Work that does not task them beyond their capabilities."

"That's insulting," Thericia muttered.

"Thericia!" Queen Jarina gasped.

Thericia could see her brother lower his head and shake it with a "not again" look, to Prince Jomin's amusement.

"Please forgive my daughter," Emperor Otias said. "She is young...and passionate."

Thericia fumed. What about Ludzenia's disparaging comment? She glared at the deputy *Primai*'s mischievous smile.

"Young passion is lovely," Ludzenia said. "Perhaps Prince Jomin would like to invite the Princess for a dance?"

Thericia knew Ludzenia only wanted to rid the table of her presence. The woman stared at her with black mesmerizing eyes. Thericia stared back as hard as she could.

The music stopped and she could hear Jomin excuse himself from his conversation with Otias.

"Would you like to dance?"

With a loud sigh, Thericia turned, found Jomin standing beside her with his hand held out, and hesitated, unsure what answer to give. The percussionist started the next song—the moment was here.

She uttered something barely intelligible. It was supposed to be "Sure." She held out her hand and he took it with a cool, firm grasp. He led her onto the floor, deep into the center of the crowd. Between her disparate thoughts of Lady Ludzenia and what her aides might have been saying to each other at their table, she remembered to keep her head up and her posture regal, a proper reflection of her father for the media.

She focused on the song as they found an opening among the dancers, quickly identifying the correct dance step to use. Alscrasian *krevoret*—syncopated rhythm, fun as long as she didn't trip over her partner's foot.

"You know the *krevoret*?" she asked Jomin.

"It's my favorite."

He smiled, their eyes met, she lost her thought. The horns jumped in, full blast, and she missed the opening steps. Jomin quickly took her hands and pivoted her to her right. With that, she found her spot and they got their rhythm. It was not the sort of stately dance that people expected from royals. She remembered to lift her skirt clear of her heels as she twirled about. At one point, she accidentally kicked into Jomin's shin, but it was only a light tap, enough for a laugh and not a wince. No doubt, the media was widecasting pictures, footage, written and narrated accounts—anything they could get out fast —throughout the imperial comm-network for rebroadcast. But it was fun, and a much better choice for dancing with the visiting Prince than a slow, serious, romantic song.

That was the next song.

The music segued, the tempo slowed, the volume diminished, and the dancers drew closer. Despite her attempts to remain nonchalant, Thericia could feel her pulse quicken and her heart beat stronger as she took his hand. She took a deep breath as a tall man in a black jacket, white shirt and pants, and gleaming silver ornaments took the microphone and began singing.

"You're a wonderful dancer," Jomin whispered. He wrapped his free arm about her and drew her in close.

Thericia struggled to calm her breathing, trying to stay relaxed. They were too close—and yet, it felt warm and comfortable.

"You sway so beautifully to the flow of the music, Princess."

"Thank you," she said.

"Would you show me around the capital, during our stay? I've read much about Alscras and the fabled views of the Great Nebula from the observatory, but have never visited until now." He smiled at her.

She could feel a rush of excitement run through her body. "I'd love to."

Prince Jomin was a pleasant surprise. Not at all like the other Alscrasian boys who had been introduced to her. This was the son of a visiting ruler. She realized that she felt a hint of jealousy, though. Here before her was a real future leader, someone who would someday follow his father's footsteps to the throne of the confederation.

She accidentally stepped on his foot. This time, she drew a wince and a painful groan. "I'm sorry! I must have lost my place."

Jomin laughed and Thericia chuckled, relieved at the break in the conversation.

The song concluded and the lights slowly brightened to a warm round of applause from the many dancers. They released their hands and she realized that her palms were completely sweaty. He let go of her waist and she started trembling. Nerves.

"Thank you for the dance, Princess."

Thericia lowered her eyes. Her mother had joked about this meeting, earlier. Could she have been right about this prince? Could she not have been joking, after all? Thericia backed away with her mind a confused jumble of conflicting emotions.

"Your Majesty—what's wrong?"

Thericia spun around at the sound of gasps.

"Oh my God!" a panic-stricken voice cried as everyone at the head table shot up from their seats.

Thericia saw a suddenly pale King Priot keel over, headfirst, onto the dining table as a crowd of attendants converged about him.

"Somebody help him!" an aide yelled.

Prince Jomin charged past her, his booming voice echoing off the back wall. "Get a doctor, fast!"

2. *Vigil*

An hour passed, the beginning of a long night of tension and worry.

Back at the palace, Thericia watched from the landing over the foyer as the Emperor hastily departed into the night with Franklen and her brother to meet with the leaders of the High Council and the star fleet commander. The sudden collapse of the *Primus* had precipitated a precarious crisis that could jeopardize the imperial peace.

She retired to her room to sit, alone, and wait for news about King Priot's condition. The *Primus* had been whisked away to the top-security hospital at Timurian star base. It was the best medical facility on the entire planet, situated just outside the capital city, where top officials and other important people were treated by the staff of the star fleet surgeon general. She assumed that Prince Jomin had also gone to the hospital to stay with his father.

Thericia looked out the window, over the city. Purplish gray clouds, reflecting the lights of the cityscape, passed overhead, obscuring the stars of the night. She struggled with her divided feelings. She worried for her father and for the empire, but surprisingly, she worried just as much for Prince Jomin. If anything happened to the *Primus*, the full weight of the confederation would come crashing down on the Prince. He was in his early twenties, but after dancing and laughing with him, Thericia could feel a youthful charm and innocence in him. He wouldn't be ready for a crisis of this magnitude.

Thericia glanced at her clock. Another hour had passed. She needed to find some news, any news, about King Priot. She buzzed for her driver, grabbed her royal blue hooded cape, and left her room, descending the grand circular staircase to the foyer.

Her mother entered the foyer from the parlor with her hands clasped. "Where are you going?"

"The hospital," Thericia said as she fastened her cape.

Queen Jarina shook her head. "No, Thericia, King Priot is guarded."

"I can pass through our security." She placed her hand on the door switch. "Royal privilege."

The Queen immediately clamped down on her hand, pulling it off the switch. "I meant the Gearmlian soldiers guarding the King's floor. You won't have clearance to pass them."

Thericia wasn't in the mood for an objection to her impromptu evening ride. "Then I'll go to the Council chamber. Father's people should have information."

"Thericia, they're in crisis meetings. Don't go bothering them."

"But it's driving me crazy, sitting here not knowing what's happening," Thericia pleaded, "and I'm worried...." She paused. Should she speak the truth? She took a deep breath. "I'm worried for Prince Jomin."

The Queen took a long look at Thericia before stepping closer. With one hand, Jarina lifted Thericia's hand; with the other, she smoothed Thericia's frazzled hair.

"Thericia," she began with a gentle voice, "try not to get swept away by the young Prince. The two of you were very courtly on the dance floor, but you are only sixteen, and he is much older, a soldier in the Gearmlian reserve."

Thericia sensed worry in her mother's voice, in her eyes. She knew where this was going. Her mother might have been joking earlier in the afternoon about her and the Prince, but she wasn't now. "I'm not being swept away, Mother."

The Queen raised an eyebrow. "No?"

Thericia shook her head. "Do you remember when Otias was in the hospital? I think he was around seven, and I was four."

Her mother didn't reply, but Thericia saw a look

of recognition in the widening of her mother's eyes.

"I was scared," Thericia continued, "and you were, too. We all were. I remember that nobody seemed to know how to cure him, and that he might...well, you know." She couldn't say the word for the ultimate end. She didn't need to. Her brother's near-fatal infection had been their darkest hour.

"Priestess Epi seemed to show up out of nowhere," Thericia said, "and she stayed with us until the doctor finally told us that Otias would be okay."

Her mother nodded. "She has always been good to us."

Thericia put her hand on her mother's arm. "The Prince is my friend. I just want to do for the Prince what Priestess Epi did for me—for us—that night."

"Thericia, he may be a friend now." The Queen gently took Thericia's hand off her arm. "You're my only daughter. I don't want you to be hurt." She looked into Thericia's eyes. "Be very, very careful with your feelings for the Prince."

Thericia nodded as the driver pulled the bronze stretch sedan into the drive-thru. It was the last of the wheeled sedans, after the previous year's replacement of the royal motor fleet with hovermobiles. Thericia didn't mind. The hovercraft were too noisy for her to concentrate on her journal writing during the long rides. "I will. If I don't learn any news at the hospital, I'll come right back."

"I think you should wait here for news."

"Mother!" Thericia glared at her mother, giving her a hard *don't treat me like a child* scowl.

Her mother sighed and released her hand.

With determination, and without further thought to her mother's warning, she greeted her driver, entered the vehicle, and took a deep breath to shake off the tense exchange.

"Where to, Your Highness?" The driver resumed his position behind the controls.

Thericia paused. Where to? She looked out the window of her vehicle, down the prominence that the palace was situated on, at the night lights of the surrounding cityscape below. The hospital, part of the vast Timurian star base outside the city, was off-limits. She saw a squadron of routine patrol craft taking off from the base as another group of similar craft landed. The State Building, and the Council chamber? The golden *serix* that topped the State Building dome cast a wide field of light from its half-dozen outstretched wings down to the surrounding office buildings. Perhaps one of Franklen's aides could see her. Thericia shook her head. Not likely.

She glanced out the opposite window, past the Temple of Lord Oscanos and Mother Gheriah, to the spaceport. There was one other possible source of information, perhaps the best source after the hospital, but one which felt unsettling to her. She took a deep breath and gave the order.

"Take me to the Gearmlian transport."

The driver recoiled. "But, Your Highness—"

"Let's go," Thericia interrupted. She waved to her mother and settled into her seat for the ride.

This time, the charcoal gray, cannon-lined Gearmlian transport felt more mysterious than anything else. A single eerie green light rotated on its topside, illuminating the oversized tail fin with each pass. The cockpit in the front was unoccupied. A pair of gray-clad soldiers, their faces hidden beneath black visors and each with a long rifle protruding from his back, stood in utter darkness, guarding the main ramp.

The driver brought the vehicle to a stop before the imposing transport. "Are they expecting you?"

Thericia shook her head. Nobody was expecting her. But she knew that, for whatever reason, the Gearmlian contingent had declined the dignitary quarters at Belltower House in favor of sleeping aboard their own military craft. "Wait here for me."

The driver's eyes bulged, his hands grabbing the back of his seat. "You're not approaching them alone?"

"It'll be all right," Thericia assured him.

"But, Your Highness—"

Thericia popped the door open and stepped out. "Wait here, I said." Like all adults her parents' age, her driver fretted too much. She straightened her cape and her hood and marched toward the two soldiers.

Surprisingly, they bowed in unison to her. "Welcome, Your Highness." The voices were slightly muffled by the visors.

"I would like to speak with Lady Ludzenia."

"She is currently unavailable," the soldier on her left said. "If you like, we could pass a message to the deputy *Primai* for you."

Thericia pursed her lips. They weren't going to get rid of her this easily. "Tell the deputy *Primai* that this is an urgent matter, and that I must speak with her immediately."

The soldier on the left bowed and disappeared into the transport, leaving the other soldier alone with her.

"We will contact the palace when the deputy *Primai* gives her reply."

Thericia stood her ground. "I'll wait for the reply."

"It may be a while."

Thericia took a deep breath. She didn't feel sleepy, not yet. It would be embarrassing if she winked out, though.

Minutes passed in silence.

"Perhaps Your Highness would prefer to stay in her vehicle," the soldier suggested.

Thericia shook her head. The driver was probably falling asleep. He wasn't supposed to, but it was late, and she was starting to feel fatigued. She didn't need a member of her own staff questioning what she was doing out here.

The soldier took the mini-com from his belt and mumbled something into it. More time passed in silence.

Finally, the other soldier returned from the bowels of the transport. "The deputy *Primai* will see you now. Please follow me."

Thericia hesitated for an instant. This was it. She glanced back at her vehicle. The driver hadn't fallen asleep. He was staring intently at her, probably worried for her safety. She considered leaving final instructions with him before heading in, but she couldn't think of anything to say. So she gave him a smile and a wave, then followed the Gearmlian soldier up the ramp and into the darkness.

The corridor inside the transport was barely lit, the walls blank, the air silent and filled with the heavy scent of lubricants. Flight systems were off. No hum of machinery, no subtle vibration in the walls. The doors had no windows, many had no markings. None had lights of any kind. Soldiers passed in silence. There was no sign of the royal guard.

Thericia had never been in a setting like this. On the one hand, she was very curious. On the other, it felt eerie. Extremely eerie. Her own bedroom felt so comfortable, and so far away.

She had never visited any of the Gearmlian worlds. She had never entered a Gearmlian setting of any kind. She only knew stories, some of which stretched back several hundred years. The most notorious were the rumors about Gearmlian mercenary soldiers. Supposedly, they weren't regular humans. Instead, they were supposed to be laboratory creations, humanoid beings with multiple arms, wings, and other strange mutations. One theory posited that they carried the preserved genes of the fabled Troggle, the reptiloid mortal enemy of the human race in the ancient Euranian myths.

Was she being stupid, entering a darkened enclosure filled with armed soldiers? She could disappear and nobody would be able to come to her rescue. She could see the looks on her parents' faces, and even that of her older brother. *Naive loose cannon does it again.* Not only would she be dead, she would be *dead*.

She shivered from the thought, but quickly reminded herself that the Gearmlians weren't their enemies. It was one big happy Central Empire, of which Alscras and the Gearmlian Confederation were the dominant political and military presences. King Priot seemed relatable enough. And Prince Jomin—well, she had danced with him. He had whispered in her ear. She had been held in his strong, comforting arms. She had flattened his toes, even. He certainly wasn't a laboratory creation. He was...no! She broke her train of thought with a deep breath and locked down her feelings. She had to stay clearheaded about this. They were rounding another corner. She had no idea where she was, within the interior of the transport, or how to get back out if she had to.

The door at the end of the corridor slid open. One shadow walked out, then another. Each seemed to walk on multiple legs. Something like a tail swung in the air behind each. Thericia could see rifles with pod-like charge-paks attached clutched in the many arms. Something unfolded and refolded behind each body as it walked. Wings? Thericia recoiled in horror, her fists clenched, her lungs hyperventilating. There really were mutant Gearmlian mercenaries...!

A third shadow stepped out. Human. Muscular. Bald. A tiny sparkling medallion hung from his neck, the only light source. Thericia recognized General Faut, the head of the Gearmlian military, who silently departed with his Gearmlian escorts in tow. Strange that he wore dark glasses in the darkness.

The door remained open a tiny slit.

"You may enter," Thericia's escort said, holding the door ajar.

So far, she was safe enough. Faut and the Gearmlian mutant soldiers disappeared around a corner, leaving her in peace. Thericia refocused on her purpose for being here. "Thank you."

The door closed behind her.

Inside, the room wasn't quite as dark as in the corridors. A pair of dim red rectangular lamps sat on the desk in the middle of the room, illuminating the green high-backed chair of a woman with her back to Thericia, closing some sort of secret cabinet. A snap sounded and the woman whirled around, her shock-white hair flaring during the spin before settling into a frazzled, static-like mess.

"Welcome, young Princess." Lady Ludzenia smiled, her blood-red lips slanting, her eyes squinting as if examining her prey, sending shivers down Thericia's spine. "What brings Your Highness before my humble presence?"

"My concern for your king," Thericia said. "I had hoped you would have news of his condition."

Ludzenia snorted. "The King is not well. There is a possibility he may not survive the night."

Thericia shivered. That was not what she had hoped to hear. She could only imagine what the implications would be for Prince Jomin. And for her father, and the empire.

"Is there anything else I may help Your Highness with?"

Thericia stood her ground. Ludzenia wasn't dismissing her this quickly. "What happened to him? Was he not well?"

Ludzenia paused, eyeing her. Thericia stared right back, her arms crossed, patiently waiting an answer.

"Very well, since you show the courtesy to inquire." Ludzenia spread her hand forward over the desk. "Please have a seat."

Satisfied that she had won this round, Thericia flipped off her hood, sat down, and made herself comfortable as the deputy *Primai* spoke.

"It is public knowledge, but rarely spoken about, that the King has a rare congenital condition known as *ghezarhiophacitis*. It is not deadly in its own right, but it does make the King vulnerable to sudden cardiac arrest from a short list of triggering causes. Depending on the trigger, it may be a mild arrest or a severe one."

Thericia knew where this was headed. Something triggered a severe arrest. Something in the food? In the air? Her mind went racing as she wondered the political ramifications of an incident on Alscrasian soil. Did she dare suspect the threat of reprisal from the confederation? "Do they know what triggered this one?" She quickly added, "I'm sure the Emperor would have given orders for dietary review and clearance when the menu was set."

Ludzenia scowled. "It *was* something the King ingested, though not necessarily from the dinner. The King takes a medication for his condition. They have not determined whether something may have interacted in his system." She glanced at the clock on her desk. "But it should not be long. There are very few other drugs which can interact with his medication."

Thericia was confused. If the King only took one medication, how could a second drug interact with it? It would have made more sense for something in the food to cause a reaction. Where was Ludzenia going with her line of discussion? Thericia paused. Was she suggesting that someone had slipped something to the King—someone Alscrasian?

"We should have a determination by the morning. Do you have any further questions?"

There was one. "I would like to visit with the Prince. Is he at the hospital with the King?"

Ludzenia tilted her head, seeming to consider Thericia's question. "Are you going to question the Prince, next?"

The question irked Thericia. This wasn't an interrogation. Not yet. "I'm only concerned for him. That's all."

"How sweet."

Thericia hated to be patronized. She doubled her resolve and waited for a proper reply to her question.

Ludzenia sighed. "Of course, the Prince is at the star base hospital. The King's condition could change at any time, in any direction."

Thericia looked down at the desk. The answer was logical and predictable, but she had still hoped that she could somehow reach the Prince. If nothing else, he might like a peer to keep him company during the long dark hours of loneliness.

Ludzenia reached into a drawer and took out a small disc. "I can see that you are very determined.

I can give you a pass to get through Gearmlian security."

Thericia's hopes jumped at the sight of the disc. Was Ludzenia really going to help her? Could even a creepy, crawly woman have a softer side? Maybe they really were one big happy Central Empire. She reached out for the disc.

Ludzenia quickly withdrew it. "I trust that we are finished, here."

So that was it. Thericia nodded, silent. She had what she wanted, and she couldn't wait to abandon the dark shadows of the troop-infested Gearmlian military transport. No doubt Ludzenia couldn't wait to get rid of the pesky young princess, either. The deputy *Primai* slowly handed the disc over.

"Thank you," Thericia said with a proper bow.

Ludzenia pressed the switch to open the door, admitting the escort soldier who had waited outside. "Good night, young Princess."

"Ever been here?" Thericia asked the driver as they approached the gate.

"No, Your Highness, this is a first for me." He flashed the royal insignia to the guard at the crossing and they were promptly waved on.

Thericia had never been to the Timurian star base before, either. She knew it wasn't a single building, but she had never imagined it to be as extensively spread out as what they drove through. The star base was like a city of its own, with not just the many expected military facilities—hangars, fuel processing, munitions processing, barracks, among others—along its perimeter, but an impressive promenade of shops, eateries, and other business establishments in its core district. Even at this late hour, a small but steady line of transport vehicles wheeled about, ferrying personnel and small equipment.

An arrangement of tall administrative buildings came into view. Thericia saw the purple ribbon logo, the insignia of the hospital, and began to feel a rush of excitement.

"Here we are," the driver said as they came to a stop before a small squad of Alscrasian soldiers.

Thericia burst out before the driver, or any of the soldiers, could let her out. "Wait for me," she said to the driver.

She showed Ludzenia's Gearmlian pass to the soldiers and was immediately escorted inside the hospital. A rapid succession of antiseptic corridors, and an endless parade of respectful salutes by the military personnel they encountered, soon brought her to a private wing and a squad of six elite Gearmlian guards. All stood at attention before an unmarked door with full body armor and helmets, a pair of sidearms and a *cuxioblade* hanging from each of their belts, and pitch black rifles protruding from their backs.

The guards saluted but remained in position to block the door.

Thericia showed them Ludzenia's pass.

The Gearmlian leader hesitated a moment, but then stepped aside, taking the others with him. "We can only allow ten minutes, Your Highness. The King is very weak."

Thericia nodded. She gently opened the door, peered into the dimly lit room, heard a slow but steady beep, and stepped in.

The first thing she saw was King Priot, lying prone and unconscious in the oversized bed. A monstrous tangle of wires connected him to an array of monitors. A spider-like medical robot stood over his head, administering three lines of medication, a web of arms simultaneously connecting it to all the monitors. She looked down the King's bed and saw Prince Jomin sitting at his feet. His head lay down on the King's legs; he was asleep. The sight touched Thericia. Jomin was obviously exhausted.

She glanced at the monitors. The cardiograph still displayed a heartbeat, though the pattern was extremely shallow and erratic. The respiration monitor was equally shallow and erratic.

The King's face was noticeably pale. Under the breathing mask, Thericia couldn't tell if his breathing was labored or not. She stepped closer and leaned over his face to get a better look. Sweat dotted his forehead. The conflicting symptoms felt all wrong to her.

Why weren't the doctors working on him? Had they given up? That would be unethical. Or had they turned everything over to the medical robot? Who was supervising the robot?

She tip-toed over to Prince Jomin and placed her hand on his shoulder. He awoke with a jolt.

"Sorry," she whispered. "I wanted to see how the King was. And how you were holding up."

Jomin looked disoriented for an instant, then he focused on his father. His brows furled and he took in a deep breath. "It's not good."

His tone of voice concerned her. She kneeled down at Jomin's side. "What did the doctor say?"

Jomin shook his head, paused for a moment, then faced Thericia, his face contorted in pain. His eyes seemed to plead for help. "They can't stabilize his heartbeat." He buried his face in his hands. "I can't lose him."

Thericia wrapped both her arms around him and held him tight. "Don't lose hope." His body trembled in her grasp. "He's still here." The moment caught her by surprise and her mind raced to think of something comforting to say while struggling with her own confused emotions for the Prince. "Every minute that passes...is another minute he's successfully held on."

Jomin quickly regained his composure and pulled away from her. "I'm sorry. My behavior is deplorable."

"No, it's not," Thericia tried to reassure him. She was both relieved and unsatisfied that the momentary bond was suddenly over. He had recaptured his formality, so she did the same. "It's perfectly understandable."

Jomin shook his head. "No, it's an embarrassment to the King." He straightened his back and cleared his voice. "A leader leads. How else could I succeed my father?"

Thericia wasn't sure it was wise to venture into this subject matter. She knew nothing about the marvels of modern medicine. There was still a chance that the King could pull through. "Please don't think bad thoughts..."

"We must be objective," he insisted, "and realistic. My father and I both knew that anything could happen at any time. That could be decades from now, or it could be tomorrow." He paused. "Or tonight."

Without warning, the medical robot withdrew its medication lines and began beeping a high-pitched signal. Alarmed, Jomin and Thericia raced to the monitors, looking for any sudden change in the data patterns. Breathing seemed unchanged. Cardiac activity was just as inconsistent as before. Brain activity was calm and still minimal. Thericia was puzzled by what could have caused the robot to withdraw.

The overhead lights came on. The door snapped open, admitting two doctors and three medical technicians. Thericia could see the Gearmlian guards standing outside the door, poised and ready for action.

"*Krok*!" the taller of the two doctors cursed as she examined the robot's data screen. Turning to the other doctor, she ordered, "Galliane, two units per second, quickly."

"What is it?" Jomin asked.

The chief doctor—Thericia saw the name "Huenio" on her name tag—glared at Jomin as the rest of the team reprogrammed and repositioned the robot. "Cepiadrine."

Jomin froze, an anguished look on his face. He swung his gaze from doctor to doctor. "How can that be?"

Thericia didn't know what Cepiadrine was. It sounded like a medication, but that was just a guess. Had someone prescribed the wrong drug? Was Galliane the correct medicine to use? Was the King now in an even more precarious situation?

"Starting," the robot said as it placed its lines into King Priot.

Dr. Huenio wiped the sweat off her forehead. "I don't know if we're in time or not."

Thericia ventured a question to Jomin. "What's Cepiadrine?" She noticed that he was trembling, shaken by what had just happened.

"It's a prescription I sometimes take for allergies on Breame...." His voice wavered and faded away.

Dr. Huenio stepped over to face Thericia. "It's usually taken in pill form, but in the Prince's case, he takes a liquid. For severe symptoms, the liquid is much faster-acting, almost instantaneous." She turned to address Jomin. "I understand that pollen in some regions of Breame can be very severe, almost life-threatening."

Jomin nodded, silent.

Thericia was still confused. "What does that have to do with the King's condition?"

Jomin heaved a sigh. "Cepiadrine can cause severe cardiac arrest in my father. I've always taken extra precautions to keep it isolated, so that there would be *no* possibility of placing him in any danger."

"Your Highness," Huenio said to Thericia, "the toxicology results we just received show traces of Cepiadrine in the King's blood. We know the cause. And what's worse, Cepiadrine is something that cannot *and should not* be treated with the Mezosil that we've been administering to the King. Mezosil not only doesn't counter the Cepiadrine, it amplifies its effects. If only we had known beforehand!" She slapped the wall, startling Thericia and everybody else.

"Doctor," one of the techs called, "we're getting a response."

Huenio, Jomin, and Thericia dashed to King Priot's side as he moaned, his eyes still closed.

"Your Majesty," Huenio called. "I'm Dr. Huenio. Can you hear me?"

No response. No detectable change in breathing, even.

Jomin leaned forward. "Father, it's Jomin." He took the King's hand. "Can you hear me? Can you squeeze my hand?"

For an instant, Thericia saw the King's eyelids move. Then, the robot's alarm sounded and the cardiac monitor went flat.

"No!" Jomin roared, embracing the King's body as the doctors rushed to prime the built-in resuscitators.

Thericia saw the brain activity monitor also go flat and knew that it was over. "Jomin." She placed her hand on his shoulder and tried to pull him away. "Do you want them to try resuscitation?"

"Yes!" He whirled about. "Do what it takes!"

"Jomin, look." Thericia pointed at the brain activity monitor.

Jomin stopped in his tracks. A single tear rolled down his cheek. "No." His voice was trembling, but clear. "The King's body must be treated with dignity and the utmost respect."

"Are you certain, Your Highness?" Dr. Huenio asked. "We're ready to proceed."

Jomin hesitated. "What is your professional opinion, Doctor?"

A sadness came over the Doctor's face as she spoke. "The King's brain activity has ceased. We can sustain his functions through artificial means. But...the natural course is to let His Majesty rest in peace. I'm terribly sorry, Your Highness."

Another tear rolled down Jomin's cheek.

"Doctor, I would like a Priest of Lord Oscanos to come administer the last rites for the *Primus*."

Dr. Huenio bowed her head. "I understand."

She directed the medical team to deactivate the resuscitators, then the entire medical team departed in silence without even attending to the shutdown of the robot or the monitors.

Alone, Thericia quickly straightened the King's sheets, then turned to the grieving Jomin. Seeing the despair in his eyes, Thericia wrapped both her arms about him and held him tight.

"I'm so sorry, Jomin," she said, softly. "If there's anything I could do for you, I would."

He wrapped his arms about her and sobbed. "I don't know how it could have happened."

"Shh, don't think about that now. Just know that your father is proud of you and your conduct in this crisis."

"Do you think so?"

"Any father would be proud of a son like you."

Jomin poured out his sorrow to Thericia, his body trembling against hers, and she wept with him.

Thericia tried her best to support him with a long, unwavering hug, the way Priestess Epi had comforted her when Otias was in the hospital. But she couldn't imagine the pain he was going through, and she suddenly became aware of her own confusion.

She hardly knew Jomin. What were her feelings for the Prince and why were they so strong? She had never lost anyone before. If something like this were to happen to her, would it be the end of her world? Was she of any help to Jomin? She could only think of the time her brother was in the hospital, and how grateful she was to Priestess Epi.

The door opened. One of the Gearmlian soldiers stepped in.

"I'm sorry, Your Highness," the soldier said.

Jomin quickly composed himself as Thericia stepped away. "It's all right, Sergeant. What do you have?"

The sergeant hesitated. Taking a deep breath, he said, "Lady Ludzenia is inquiring about the *Primus*."

Thericia and Jomin looked at each other with hesitant eyes.

The sergeant, glancing at the body and the flatlined monitors, stiffened momentarily, then took a step toward Jomin. "My most sincere condolences, Your Highness. You are now the interim monarch of Breame." He signaled the rest of the Gearmlian soldiers to step in. Together, they took a deep, slow bow. "We stand ready to escort you back to the transport."

Jomin looked to Thericia, acting unsure.

"Please give him a few minutes," she quickly said to the sergeant. "The Prince could never have imagined this happening to his father."

"No." Jomin took a deep breath and shook his head. Now in a solid, commanding voice, he said, "I need to inform Lady Ludzenia about this matter."

Memories of her recent encounter with the deputy *Primai* suddenly surfaced in Thericia's head. She grabbed his arm. "Wait."

"This can't wait," he said, pulling his arm from her grasp. "The confederation needs me." He paused and glanced at the King's face. Slowly, he bent down and gave his father a gentle kiss on the back of the hand.

As Jomin rose to leave with the sergeant, Thericia quickly grasped his arms. "Don't go."

His face twisted with a confused look. "What?"

She quickly held her tongue and eyed the sergeant, unsure if she was treading into subject matter she shouldn't.

Jomin's face changed into a look of concern. "What is it?"

Thericia summoned her resolve, stepped closer, and lowered her voice. "I don't trust Lady Ludzenia."

Jomin pulled back. His eyes narrowed. He spoke through clenched teeth. "What are you saying?"

Thericia wasn't sure why, but Lady Ludzenia felt dangerous to her. The Prince was brave and honorable, perhaps too much so. He would be completely defenseless and alone, surrounded by soldiers, both human and not, who reported to the mysterious General Faut. She wanted to believe that he could hold his own against Ludzenia, but her instincts told her otherwise.

"You're wrong about her," Jomin said, pushing her away. "She's a very capable official and a loyal aide to my father. Do you know that many of the confederation's reforms were her initiatives? Production increases, military jobs, R&D, religious outreach, there's more. Gearmlian standing in the empire has improved under her watch."

Thericia lowered her head, saddened that she had upset Jomin. "I'm sorry. If there is anything I can do to help...."

Jomin shook his head and turned to follow the sergeant.

"I can stay with your father until the priest arrives," Thericia offered. For what it was worth, she could help him at least this much.

Jomin stopped when he reached the door and nodded in silence.

"When will I hear from you?" she asked. "How will I hear from you?"

"I don't know."

After Jomin and the others departed, Thericia sat alone in the hospital room with the body of the late King of Breame and her many thoughts.

Interlude

The death of King Priot had thrown the confederation, and the empire, into uncertainty. What could a sixteen-year-old girl do to help? She knew too little about imperial politics to venture even a single passing thought. But worse, where her mind should have been focused on the affairs of her father, it now wandered to other concerns. The Prince and his needs.

Thericia knew that she needed help from the one person who could help counsel her with her predicament: Priestess Epi. She only hoped that her former teacher wouldn't mind being woken up in the middle of the night.

She stared out her window at the twinkling stars of the Alscrasian sky. After departing the star base, her sedan wound its way through the metropolis, the driver maintaining his silence as they traveled. If he disagreed with her course of action, he kept it to himself. That was a good thing. Too many conflicting thoughts crowded her mind to consider going home, yet.

She had not visited the Gherian Garden Convent in over two years, only once since her graduation from the primary novice school. She still received brief calls from Priestess Epi once every three or four months. Thericia made it a point to send her former guardian priestess a gift twice every year: on Creation Day, and on the first day of the annual *Celebrian* Festival, which marked the liberation of the human race from the dark lord Luzomi. But in person, it had been too long. As they climbed the temple mount toward the convent grounds, Thericia both felt excited with anticipation and mentally scolded herself for being too lazy to make this visit much earlier. She just had to remember not to stay too late. It would be a long ride, and she had told her mother her impromptu visit would be a brief one.

Needing to organize her thoughts, Thericia reached into the folds of her cape, brought out her pocket-com, and began writing.

"It's a long ride to the convent, and I have to be honest with someone...."

Thericia paused to consider her words carefully.

"I've never felt for anyone what I'm feeling for him.

"His loneliness, his need, his sorrow, his pain.

"He feels real, he's not some far-off prince.

"I need to help him."

Thericia could already see that her train of thought was spiraling into an emotional roller coaster. She took a breath to clear her head and try to approach it a little more rationally.

"I know my mother's wise and I'm young (and foolish?), but we're not the same.

"I want to be involved. I know I can help.

"I can't stay home while our world changes."

She stopped again and looked out the window. The pink bead lights of the convent, peeking out from beyond the passing trees then disappearing behind an overhanging rock, tantalized her.

They rounded a narrow curve in the mountain pass until the road leveled out. Then, she saw the massive arch that welcomed visitors to the lush, park-like plateau, and the temple of Mother Gheriah, the creator of the human race. Fountains decorated the grounds, each decorated with a con-tinuously-changing display of soft lights. Directly ahead, at the top of a flight of wide stone steps, stood the massive stone temple, fronted by an array of twenty-foot tall colonnades and a pair of ten-foot Alscrasian multi-winged *serix* statues. From the back of the roof, the smokestack emitted a wispy column of reddish smoke rising from the ever-burning Creation Cauldron.

She was nearing her destination. Was she ready to share her most intimate needs?

"Feelings are feelings, whatever they may be.

"Nothing right or wrong about them, as long as they're genuine from the heart.

"Mine is..."

She jerked her stylus off the screen. She couldn't go further. Not now. Not when she wasn't sure what her deepest feelings really were.

Thericia's attention riveted to the two story rectangular building to the temple's right. Surrounded by a series of manicured gardens, it was the convent where the temple priestesses lived, where young Thericia had spent the majority of her school years. They had been happy years. There had been occasional moments of challenge and frustration, but they had always been short, followed by warmth and comfort from her favorite teacher, Priestess Epi.

They pulled into the deserted drive-thru and the driver promptly helped Thericia out. It was the dead of night, but matters were urgent.

After the young novice brought Thericia through a short hallway to a small sitting room, she left. Thericia walked around the simple furniture—a small table, two cushioned chairs, and a settee—and passed the time gazing at the inspiring art work on the walls. A romanticized painting of Mother Gheriah, dressed in flowing red robes, with a long white bonnet over her golden hair and a gentle smile on her ruby red lips. Her messenger to the humans, young pixie-like Jhoraine, full of feathery wings over her ears, elbows, and ankles. Heroic

Lord Oscanos, savior of the human race, with his skin a gleaming green and his mighty muscles bulging. The mysterious Guardians of the Past, Future, and the Multiverse, three alluring women who were part avian and part marine, part young and beautiful, and part aged and decrepit. They kept safe the foundational structure of the physical universe.

As a child who grew up in the convent school, Thericia never ceased to marvel at the wonder of the Euranian Ancestors, the almighty deities of all creation. Looking at these beautiful depictions, she still felt the mind-boggling awe of the ancient tales. How Mother Gheriah created Euae, the first woman, then her seven children, including Gor, the first son. How Lord Oscanos defended the human race from the heinous Luzomi and led the great Adelph and the surviving humans to their new home worlds. How long ago all those happened, no one knew. But as Priestess Epi had constantly reminded young Thericia, mystery was what reminded everyone that life itself was miraculous.

"Your Highness!"

Priestess Epi stood at the doorway, looking extremely aged with a slightly hunched posture and wispy gray hair peeking out from under her black headdress, but with a wide smile and a bright twinkle still in her eye. Thericia instinctively ran over and embraced her former guardian Priestess.

"I'm sorry it's taken me so long to come back to

visit you," Thericia said.

"You'll say no such thing," Priestess Epi said. "I'm so glad to see you." She lowered her voice. "Even if the hour is an odd one."

Thericia lowered her eyes, embarrassed for waking the elderly priestess in the dead of night. A member of the royal family should have the well-being of the people foremost in their minds. It was an axiom that Thericia had committed to memory, but that didn't happen, this time. Thericia was entirely consumed by the Prince and his predicament. She hadn't come to visit her beloved friend, the Priestess. Instead, she had come to ask her for help, the same way that she had, countless times during her schooling.

Priestess Epi's hand gently lifted Thericia's chin. Their eyes met.

"What is it, child?"

Thericia trembled, but not because of nerves from reuniting with Priestess Epi. She reminded herself that she was coming of age and no longer a child easily scared. Taking a deep breath, she whispered, "Priestess Epi, I think...I might be...I care for someone. Someone dealing with the death of his father, and all that entails."

Priestess Epi closed her eyes and nodded with understanding.

Thericia quickly stammered, "It might be...nothing. But I can't but feel that he needs me." Catching her breath, she saw the twinkle in Priestess Epi's eyes, again.

"Come."

Thericia followed Priestess Epi down a short hall to a small parlor, where she was directed to sit in a plain but comfortable settee while Priestess Epi switched on a lamp and dispensed hot water.

"Among the greatest mysteries of life," Priestess Epi said, handing Thericia a dainty, flower-shaped cup of aromatic herbal tea, "is that of the bond between male and female." She joined Thericia on the settee, taking a quiet sip of her own tea. "It is a mystery that is paramount to our existence. You have already learned the facts of life, but experiencing this is something you cannot be prepared for."

Thericia, after filling Priestess Epi in on all that had transpired between her and the Prince, was back in the classroom again, a young student enchanted by the lessons of her teacher, absorbing every word like a sponge. She forgot about her tea.

"Do you remember the tale of Euae and her children?"

Thericia nodded and began reciting from memory.

"The sun lowered and the air cooled and fell silent. The sun rose and the air warmed and filled with the sounds and songs of life. Again, the sun lowered and the air cooled and fell silent. And again, the sun rose and the air warmed and filled with the sounds and songs of life.

"And a low voice spoke, its words echoing about: 'Behold, your mother.'

"And the Oracle of J'horaine lifted her head. In the morning light, the ancient jewels of the pool began to sparkle. Rainbow colors filled the clearing with animated life. Brilliant lights reflected in the waters of the pool. The mists in the air swirled about an image of a woman, emerging from the pool to stand before her. And the Oracle recognized the hunched figure of Euae, whose dark, straggly, body-length strands covered her naked body, the fabled mother of the human race.

"The mists in the air swirled about the Oracle of J'horaine and formed an image of seven people— some tall, some short, some lying in a ball— positioned before her.

"These are the names of Eaue's offspring.

"The first child was named Aia, and she grew in the image of her mother.

"The second child was named Boh, and she grew in the image of her mother.

"The third child was named Ka, and except for her unusual pale hair color, she grew in the image of her mother.

"The fourth child was named Seih. She did not grow much hair. Nor did she grow much at all, remaining small in stature and unable to walk or stand erect, as her older sisters did.

"The fifth child, and the first to die, was named Ta.

"The sixth child, and the second to die, was named Oau.

"The seventh child, the troublesome one, was named Gor. Over time, he learned to be calm and cooperative with his sisters, and he grew to be much larger and stronger than everyone else."

Thericia was amazed she still remembered all the names and descriptions. She quickly decided it was because she had had a good teacher.

"How Gor came to be born is one of the greatest mysteries." Priestess Epi took a sip. "He was different—physically, emotionally, intellectually. He had a different temperament and a different view. It was as if he was similar on the outside, but an entirely different being on the inside."

Thericia nodded. "He was a boy, the first one."

"He confused his mother and fought with his sisters, aggravating everyone. He incited the ancient flying Xoths, and their razor-sharp teeth and claws left him in a bloody mess that his mother and sisters had to nurse back to health." Priestess Epi put her cup down, a serious look now in her eyes. "But he survived a prolonged childhood and grew tall and strong. Through him, the propagation of the human race came into being. We stand here, today, a great multitude blanketing the many worlds of Eurania, because of his existence. When he gave his life in the fight against the terrible Troggle, the reptilian creation of Luzomi and the mortal enemy of the human race, he saved his offspring from total annihilation. He became our first defender." Priestess Epi lowered her head and bowed her head in reverence.

Thericia had heard the story before, as a child. Now, she listened with the mind of a young adult on the verge of womanhood.

"But why was he so?" Priestess Epi paused, allowing Thericia a moment to ponder the story. "Why was he different? How were the women to understand someone such as him?" She smiled. "How men and women 'fit together' is beyond all comprehension. They just do."

Thericia thought she understood. "That's why I feel as if the Prince and I should be together, even though it's so confusing that my head hurts?"

"Perhaps." Priestess Epi placed her hands on Thericia's shoulders. "Only you can decide if that is how you will interpret your feelings. We will never know, for sure. We can only experience it."

Thericia felt better, but Priestess Epi hadn't addressed how to help the Prince, yet.

Thericia watched Priestess Epi rummage through a small box that she had taken from a drawer in the table, her mind focused on the Prince and his meeting with Lady Ludzenia. Why was she so concerned about his wellbeing, and whether he could stand up to the deputy *Primai*? It was comforting to know that it was a timeless feeling, that others had walked in her shoes before her, that she wasn't alone with the chaos rumbling about within her. But what should she do?

Priestess Epi brought out a small ring and held it out to Thericia. "This is for you."

Thericia took it and examined it. The design was abstract, an arrow twisting through and between two intertwined red stones. "It's beautiful, and bizarre." She was captivated by it, and at the same time, somewhat confused.

"How men and women fit together is beyond comprehension," Priestess Epi reminded her. "They just do. You are at the beginning of a beautiful, and at times bizarre, journey. My counsel to you is to be patient and let it evolve naturally until it finds a home in your heart. In the meantime, you have much life to live, experience, and enjoy."

"Thank you." Thericia gave Priestess Epi a heartfelt hug.

"What are you going to do, now?"

Thericia looked to Priestess Epi. "What do you think I should do?"

"I think you should go home, rest, and wait."

That was not the answer Thericia had hoped for. "I can't do that."

Priestess Epi raised an eyebrow. "Why not?"

Thericia swallowed hard. The urgency of the situation should have been obvious. "The Prince needs someone by his side during this crisis."

"I understand your concern and your viewpoint." Priestess Epi tilted her head. "But you hardly know the Prince."

Thericia looked down at the floor. "I saw his anguish. His tears." She gripped Priestess Epi's arm. "You remember the time my brother was in the hospital, fighting for his life, don't you? It meant everything to me that you were with us. I just want to do the same for the Prince. I was there when his father died. He's forced to suppress his loneliness so that he can get to work with Lady Ludzenia." Thericia looked into Epi's eyes, hoping for any help her Priestess could give.

Priestess Epi placed her hand on Thericia's shoulder. "I do remember. But this is different. Your brother was a child, and so were you. If the King is dead, then the Prince is now the interim monarch. He is a grown man and must show himself a worthy leader, lonely as it is. It is, in fact, a reality you may need to face, some day."

Thericia's jaw dropped. She couldn't believe what she was hearing.

Epi nodded. "Your feelings for him are transparent. They, not rational thoughts, are driving your decisions. That is not worthy of a Princess."

The words struck Thericia like a scolding from her father, who was always mindful of her conduct as a royal. Priestess Epi was like a third parent.

"Have you progressed in your education of your father's dealings?" Epi continued without pause, her tone held steady. "If anything were to happen—and let us pray that nothing will—but if it did, could you step into a larger, more important role in the life of the empire?"

Thericia lowered her eyes.

"If you take a deep breath and consider my point of view, I think you would agree with me that you are being steered astray by your attraction to the Prince. In all honesty, there are more important matters for your attention."

Thericia defiantly shook her head. She was only supporting someone in need, nothing more. Priestess Epi was imagining something that wasn't there. "But—"

"You should go home and wait." Epi's voice was not loud, but it was firm, nevertheless. "If the Prince calls for you, he will try to contact you there."

It took great effort, but Thericia managed to stifle the urge to protest further. She trusted Priestess Epi. She knew she should be thankful for her frank advice, which included a very good point. Somebody had slipped the King the wrong drug. Who? But as she turned to depart, Thericia couldn't hide her feelings of disappointment and discouragement toward all the adults.

3. The Hidden Realm

Upon returning to the palace, Thericia dismissed the driver with a quick word of thanks and headed back up to her room. Her mother met her at the top of the grand staircase.

"Any news from father?" she asked the Queen.

"Only a brief note from Mr. Franklen." Queen Jarina looked concerned but calm. "They are discussing the turn of events. It may be a while before your father returns."

No doubt, a lot of people were working through the night, by now. "Is there anything I can do?"

Queen Jarina shook her head. "It's now an internal matter of the confederation." She pointed a finger at Thericia. "It's a good thing for your father, and for the empire as a whole, assuming things can be skillfully worked out."

"Is it?" Thericia couldn't believe what she had heard. "You yourself said you don't trust Lady Ludzenia. Can't you see that she's going to become the next leader of the confederation if we don't help the Prince?"

"We can't intervene in their internal affairs," Queen Jarina said. "It could jeopardize the peace between Alscras and the Gearmlians. Surely, you can see that it can't be good, no matter how you look at it."

"But—"

"Think of the good of our people, Thericia," Queen Jarina insisted.

Thericia grimaced, her fists tight with tension. Her heart wanted to help the Prince, but her head agreed with her mother. She remembered Priestess Epi's advice. As difficult as it was, she knew she should heed their words. She obediently nodded her head, acknowledging her understanding of the situation. "I'm just...tired."

"You've had a long night," the Queen said. "Try to get some rest."

"Yes, mother." She gave her mother a hug and, after receiving a kiss on the forehead, retired to her room.

After cleaning up and changing, she stood before her bedside table altar, a modest porcelain arrangement that included a primitive thatch-roofed house with Mother Gheriah and her aides standing before a cobalt blue Cauldron of Creation. A figurine of Jhoraine, the messenger to the people, flew over the house, a sweeping rainbow trailing behind her.

Taking a slow deep breath to calm her thoughts and her feelings, she quietly said her evening prayers, being mindful to limit her supplications to only those that she was truly in need of. In this instance, guidance and direction in dealing with her feelings for the Prince. Most nights, she prayed without real expectation of a reply. But tonight was different. Tonight, she asked for an answer. Then, she went to bed, closed her eyes, and waited.

And a dream entered her sleep.

Shadows and a thick stench of foul odors surrounded her. Invisible tentacles snaked past her and giant wings fluttered over her. She was standing in an underground cavern. Cold water rose to cover her feet. It inched up her legs until it reached her waist. She opened her eyes and looked down at the thick red liquid that surrounded her. A dark brown fin protruded from the water. Two rows of sharp spikes brushed each of her legs. A bony black hand rose from the water, holding an eyeball. A voice spoke in her mind.

'For you, my lovely child.'

It was the dreaded Wa'ohl'thu, the keeper of souls, a shadowy being who ruled over Xemahb, the underverse, where the lost among the departed wandered without direction or purpose.

Thericia looked at the eye, and it radiated a rainbow of colors, illuminating the cavern. The reflecting pool sparkled in brilliant color. It felt very comfortable, as if she were standing in the heat of a midday sun.

And then, a second hand emerged with a small mirror and she gazed at her reflection in it. She saw herself in a white dress that draped into the water, with a garland of tiny pink flowers over her head like a crown, and a sparkling green and gold brooch that accented a short silver necklace. And in the background of her reflection, among the jagged rock formations that lined the walls of the cavern, she saw an image of Lady Ludzenia standing over the unconscious body of the Prince.

Thericia awoke with a jolt, bathed in cold sweat. For an instant, she wasn't sure whether she had screamed or not. Her whole body trembled. She reached over and took her bedside glass of water, downing all the contents without pause. She squeezed her eyes shut, took deep breaths, and waited for her nerves to calm. It was only a dream. Only a dream. A dream. Have no fear, she told herself, no fear. After passage of a minute or two, with no one appearing to check on her, she finally concluded that she hadn't audibly screamed.

She leaned forward and rested with the temples of her forehead on her hands. It had seemed so real, but she knew that the images couldn't have been real. The Wa'ohl'thu was a figure from the mythical past. Of all the Euranian Ancestors, it alone had no anecdotes of sightings or miraculous visions. It alone brought forth ambiguous feelings—questions of whether it was evil or not, whether the under-verse was hellacious or not, and what its relationship with True Eurania, the mythical world of origin where the souls of the blessed basked in the love and joy of Almighty Euranus for all eternity, was.

Thericia couldn't sleep. Could the Prince be in danger? She couldn't even close her eyes. The stillness of the night spooked her. She threw her covers aside and got out of bed, restless. She peered out the window. Dark and quiet. A few sky vehicles flew overhead, but traffic along the major land routes was sparse.

Should she wake her driver back up? She shook her head. It had been a long night for both of them and it felt cruel to rob him of his rest further. The sedan engine would also break the quiet of the night. She had nothing concrete to go on, just a feeling about Lady Ludzenia. She told herself to dismiss this feeling, but somewhere in the back of her head, a soft solitary voice told her to heed her intuition. Her mother relied on her intuition, and she was often proved correct. This hunch about the deputy *Primai*'s designs on the Prince was a stretch, but one she couldn't brush off. It stuck in her head. Ludzenia was dangerous, and the Prince could soon be in trouble—if he wasn't, already.

She couldn't sit around. More than anything, Thericia had to find out what was happening. She dug through her closet for the darkest, stealthiest outfit in her wardrobe. Donning a black hooded cape and a pair of black pants, she quietly headed down-stairs, tip-toeing so that she wouldn't wake her mother or any of the staff. She descended the back stairs, past the domestic staff quarters, and out to the compound.

The soft sounds of the night—the hums of the nocturnal traffic, the buzz of the overhead craft, the rustle of the tree leaves within the compound swaying in the intermittent breeze—both calmed her nerves and heightened her senses. Her footsteps over the colorful tile pavement sounded far too loud to avoid waking somebody up. When she reached the finely manicured lawn, her steps softened considerably, and she quickened her pace, walking past the groundskeeper's quarters, the workshop, the storage units, the garage, and the grains bins, until she reached the little stable.

"Torrey?" Thericia whispered, stepping inside.

She quickly walked over to the mound of hair among the pile of leaves in the rear corner, being mindful to leave the light off. She winced as each step brought a loud crunch of leaves under her foot. Without warning, a pair of large ears popped up and a head lifted. Thericia quickly reached over and held the animal's long snout to prevent him from letting out a cry.

"Shhh," she whispered in his floppy ear. "It's me." She gave him a quick kiss on the hairy forehead. "Don't be frightened."

He turned his head to look at her with his large,

bulbous eyes, sniffed several times, then lowered his head and nudged her face with his cheek.

"Sorry to wake you up," she said, "but I need your help." She quickly and quietly brushed the leaves off his back. Letting go of his snout, she brought Torrence to his feet. "Come."

The *haissen* stood on all fours and followed her to the door. Thericia quickly fastened the riding saddle and attached the reins, looping them around his muscular shoulders. She then peeked through the door and surveyed the palace grounds in her view. A lone security guard strolled about.

Thericia let out a quiet exhale. "We'll have to wait a minute, Torrey."

Torrence peeked through the door, also, and blew out his breath.

"Shh!" Thericia whispered, grabbing the snout again. "Not so loud. Okay?" She patted Torrery's head, stroking and smoothing his hair over his forehead.

The *haissen* stared at her, then nodded its head.

Thericia peeked out the door again, watching the security guard and patiently waiting for him to disappear behind the equipment barn. Just as the guard reached the corner of the building, he stopped, turned back, and reached into his pocket, lifting something to his face. He then lit a small flame and started a *cuira* stick, blowing out a puff of light gray smoke, before continuing on his route, finally rounding the corner and disappearing behind the equipment barn.

This was it, Thericia realized. She could still change her mind, take the saddle off, and put Torrence back to bed. Once she rode out, she would be committed. She would run the risk of ending up in the sights of the deputy *Primai* of the Gearmlian Confederation, a position Prince Jomin was already in.

She was only sixteen. Her future lay before her. But what was that future to be? She was not involved in the world of interstellar politics, as her brother was. She was like a younger version of her mother, staying home day after day, finding ways to make herself useful to the empire.

Was she prepared to leave the comfort of her circle of attendants and their trivial pursuits to join the Prince, wherever he was? Priestess Epi had advised her to wait for the Prince to contact her.

The Emperor—her father—would never approve of this course of action. If he knew.

Thericia gazed at Torrence, who stood at attention, awaiting whatever direction she decided to follow, and felt amazed that she could command an independent, intelligent being as she did. She could give the order to return to bed, and Torrey would. Or, she could give the order to venture out into the night, and he would. Did she truly belong in her parlor, in the midst of her circle of handmaidens, or did she belong in a bigger world? The more she pondered, the more confused she became, both about the immediate decision and the long term ramifications. One thing she knew, though.

"If I don't help the Prince," she said to Torrence, "Lady Ludzenia will become the leader of the confederation. That would mean trouble for my father, and for the empire."

She looked out the door, this time at the larger world outside, and with slow steps, led Torrence out of the stable. "Let's go."

This time, the Gearmlian transport looked like a prison, nearly pitch black and surrounded by guards who paced back and forth with their rifles in hand. Thericia did her best to keep both herself and Torrence out of sight, behind a collection of starter fuel barrels. As she watched, a pair of Gearmlian guards in metallic gear strolled into sight. They each carried a rifle in casual fashion over their shoulder as they paced back and forth before the darkened main ramp.

Thericia strained to listen as the two guards spoke in low tones.

"...Prince...." one seemed to say.

The Prince? She could see the other shaking his head.

"...information...." the second said.

She wanted to sneak closer. Perhaps she could pick up a few more words.

"...fate...."

Thericia couldn't tell which guard had uttered

the last word. Suddenly, she gasped, a black feeling of horror threatening to engulf her. Something ominous, something involving Lady Ludzenia? The Prince's fate? She must have misheard, from this distance. She held onto Torrey's neck to steady herself. Would she dare approach the guards and seek re-admittance?

The rear ramp of the transport lowered. A long, sleek black vehicle, with its lights on but very dim, and its passenger bubble blackened, drove out and pulled up before the main ramp. Two regular Gearmlian soldiers climbed out and stood at attention as another pair of similar soldiers walked down the ramp. A third figure followed closely behind with a long robe flowing like a fluttering tail.

Lady Ludzenia, departing for somewhere in the middle of the night.

Thericia tensed. She didn't have time to ponder her decision. Ludzenia and her soldiers climbed in. The sliding door closed. A short stabilizing tail raised from the body, and the hover-mobile lifted off and whisked away from the transport.

She couldn't think of a reason why Ludzenia would leave the transport in the middle of the night, unless it was for a clandestine purpose. With a hard pull on the saddle, she sprang up on Torrence's back.

"Go!"

Torrence reared up on his hind legs, lifting Thericia high into the air, and they dashed away into the night, in pursuit.

Within minutes, they departed the star base. Ludzenia's vehicle made an unexpected turn away from the city and sped into the distance.

"Come on!" Thericia ordered Torrence, who lowered his head and charged even faster on his four powerful legs.

The hovercraft soon left the main road and followed a single-lane path up into the hills. When Thericia tried to steer Torrence onto the same path, the *haissen* reared back and shook his head, grunting a vehement protest. Thericia felt Torrence start trembling. She watched the dim lights of Ludzenia's vehicle continue on, disappearing into the woods for a moment before reappearing higher up the path.

They were heading into the barren hills of Zemuir, the reputed home of pixies, *Venot* sprites, and other strange spiritual beings that populated the stories that Alscrasian parents told their children. She had never taken Torrence in, never taken him anywhere close. *He* was spooked, and she knew that animal instincts were much more trustworthy than human instincts.

Ludzenia was growing more mysterious by the minute.

"Come on, Torrey." Thericia stroked his neck with determination. "Don't be afraid. We'll be all right. I promise you."

Torrence lowered his forelegs and shook his head.

Thericia took a deep breath. "No, Torrey." She

spoke with a stern tone. "We have to go. Now." She gave the reins a firm, uncompromising pull.

Torrence protested, but she successfully turned him toward the hills.

"Go."

With that, the *haissen* obeyed, and they headed into the hills, following the still-visible lights of the vehicle. As she rode, Thericia could feel slight touches on her shoulders, ostensibly from the wind or the leaves. She kept her focus ahead, though. By conveying confidence, Thericia strengthened Torrence's resolve to venture deeper into the unknown.

Soon, they exited the other side of the woods and began climbing the succession of rolling hills under the moonlight. At first, the ground was covered in tall, dry grasses that swept against them as they ran past. Then, the grasses thinned and they reached barren ground, hard rock with layers of dirt and dust that encrusted at the base of the sparse, bush-like vegetation that sprang up here and there. Long spikey reeds extended from the bushes, ball-like bulbs permeated throughout the stems of the bizarre shrubs.

They climbed over a mound—and Thericia pulled Torrence to a sudden stop with a hard yank. Dead ahead sat the black hover-mobile, grounded and silent but with its lights still on, completely deserted. Thericia hopped off Torrence and pushed him down to lay flat on his stomach, his head on the ground, as much out of sight behind the formation of bushes as possible.

"Shh," she whispered.

She hid behind Torrence's body and watched the vehicle, which sat about twenty-five yards away, waiting for Ludzenia or the soldiers to appear.

Nothing.

Then, a light appeared on the other side of the vehicle. It was a strange blue glow that pulsated very slowly. Torrence lifted his head. Thericia quickly grabbed his snout and calmed him with firm, even strokes down his neck, until he lowered his head back down. "Stay here."

Stepping out from behind Torrence body, she sneaked over to the deserted vehicle and hid behind it, listening. A low, raspy voice spoke.

"Come to me, O Keeper of Souls,

"Make your presence known.

"Enter this realm and claim your throne,

"Come to me, I beseech thee."

Lady Ludzenia—chanting? The "Keeper of Souls" was the dreaded Wa'ohl'thu—the same deity that had haunted her dream.

Was this another dream, or was it real?

Thericia peeked over the tail of the vehicle and saw the backside of the flame-red robe that flowed down from Lady Ludzenia's head of ghost-white hair. Partially hidden from Thericia's sight by Ludzenia's body was the glowing blue light. She could see reeds, similar to the surrounding vegetation, extend upward from the ground. Was the light a pixie?

"The touch of life, to the touch after life."

Ludzenia hunched lower and lower toward the light, her voice turning into more of a growl than the clear annunciation she normally used. Thericia shivered from a sudden flash of wild thoughts about the deputy *Primai*—could she have a hidden persona?

"The son of your latest, I offer to you.

"The young and handsome, to feed your hunger."

Thericia gasped at what she heard. The young and handsome could only be....she clenched her fists. Deputy *Primai* Ludzenia wanted to offer him to the Lord of the underworld? Thericia swung her gaze from side to side, searching her surroundings. Where was Jomin being kept? Surely, he had to be somewhere nearby.

"I humbly ask your will for me.

"Make me your vessel, empower me.

"I will gather all of this realm for you."

Ludzenia bowed low to the ground and Thericia caught sight of a blue luminous being extending itself from the bush. She began to feel faint. She quickly put her hands on the vehicle and took deep breaths. The reeds parted and skeletal arms and fingers emerged, covered with eyeballs of all shapes, sizes, and colors that turned about in all directions.

The far-reaching, all-seeing Wa'ohl'thu.

Thericia had never seen it before. She forced

herself to cover her mouth to keep from screaming. It wasn't a human figure like the Mother Gheriah or Jhoraine statuettes, nor was it bestial like the depictions of evil Luzomi or his lieutenants. It was a *thing*, a creepy, crawly, freak of nature like no other, more of a carnivorous plant than an intelligent being. Did it have a brain? A line of incisors rose from the middle of the bush.

It was all Thericia could do to keep from retching at the sight of the undulating limbs that jutted back and forth. This was the keeper of people's souls? It was a monster.

She heard Torrence cry out. She spun around to face the two Gearmlian soldiers who now stood between her and her *haissen* with their rifles aimed.

4. *The Mercenary*

"Well, what do you have to say for yourself?"

Lady Ludzenia squinted at Thericia, raised her arm at one of the soldiers, and snapped her fingers. The soldier raised his *cuxioblade* and smacked Torrence in the hindquarters with the flat side, sending the *haissen* running away into the night with a yelp.

"No!" Thericia cried out, collapsing to her knees.

"Get up!" Ludzenia ordered. "Your conduct is unbecoming."

Alone, surrounded by the desolate scrub brush of the wilderness, and flanked by the two armed soldiers, young Thericia stood before Lady Ludzenia, struggling to keep from crying. She had never felt scared for her life like this before.

Why didn't she listen to Priestess Epi and wait in her room? Why did she have to act so impulsively? She could only silently curse herself for being so stupid.

Ludzenia squinted at Thericia. "I trust you realize the gravity of your situation, young Princess."

Pushed into a corner, Thericia could only try to seize the offensive. "You can't hold me! You don't have the authority, here."

"Oh, but I do," Ludzenia corrected. She slowly walked around Thericia, her black boots crunching dry twigs with each step.

"My father will come get me," Thericia countered. "You're on our planet, not yours."

"My military transport is sovereign territory." Ludzenia stepped closer, until she was barely a foot away from Thericia. Her jet black eyes stabbed at Thericia, hot air emitting through her fiery red lips. "Once we return, you will be on foreign soil, the same as if you had journeyed to a confederation planet." She smiled. "Your father cannot enter a Gearmlian vessel without receiving an official invitation from me. Or without declaring war."

Thericia's heart sank.

Ludzenia nodded to the soldiers. "Let us return to safe haven." Throwing a scowl at Thericia, the deputy *Primai* whirled about, her hair flaring like a thousand pointed bristles, and entered the vehicle.

The soldiers then pulled the struggling Thericia toward the vehicle.

"Let me go!" she yelled.

One of the soldiers pulled out a pair of thick

metal handcuffs and fastened her hands together behind her back.

"No!"

After opening the front door, they shoved her inside and quickly sandwiched her in the front seat between them. Ludzenia, meanwhile, sat alone in the back.

Overpowered and squeezed tight by the weight of the cold metal armor the soldiers wore, Thericia quieted down for the smooth but swaying ride back to the transport. She hated this hovercraft. It made her stomach sick. As they descended the hills, Thericia could only think about her father, and how much she missed the safety and security of the palace.

Nobody even knew she was here.

Maybe the wretched Ludzenia wouldn't harm her. Maybe the woman was just mad that Thericia had witnessed her doing whatever it was that she was doing with Wa'ohl'thu. Maybe...but deep down, Thericia knew the reality of it all: Ludzenia was a woman harboring deep secrets.

They soon came into view of the black transport. It still looked like a prison—now, her prison. Thericia couldn't decide whether it was best to throw up a strong resistance all the way or feign resignation. She didn't know what to do.

The guards marched down the main ramp and opened the hovercraft doors.

Ludzenia addressed her soldiers, "Inform

General Faut we have a guest." Glancing at Thericia, she added, "A visiting dignitary, of sorts." Ludzenia then brushed past the guards and headed up the ramp, disappearing into the darkness.

One of the soldiers gave Thericia's arm a strong pull. "This way," he barked, yanking her up the ramp with them.

Inside, she followed the soldiers through the same silent, darkened corridors that she had walked earlier that evening. At that time, she had been scared of venturing into an unknown setting, surrounded by unknown people from an area of the empire that she had never seen. Now, she feared for her life, and she realized that the sick feeling in her stomach wasn't just from the ride. Raw desperation gnawed at her gut. They soon passed Ludzenia's door and entered a new corridor. Now, she could really disappear and nobody would be able to come to her rescue.

The door at the end of the unfamiliar corridor slid open. One shadow walked out, then another. Each walked on multiple legs. A tail swung in the air behind each. Thericia could see rifles clutched in the many arms. Wings unfolded and refolded behind each body as it walked. Thericia struggled to keep from hyperventilating. Two of the mutant Gearmlian mercenaries, again.

To her horror, the soldiers brought her before the towering monstrous beings and handed her off to them.

"You may enter," Thericia's initial escort said before departing.

She nearly cried out as one of the mercenaries grasped her arm with its clammy, suction-like hand and pulled her into the darkened room.

Inside, she found herself standing before an expansive desk with a built-in light that shone upward, illuminating the olive-green uniform of its occupant—a bald, muscular man whose face was hidden behind a handheld porta-com, a tiny sparkling medallion hanging from his neck. The man lowered the porta-com, and as the door behind her slammed shut, Thericia recognized Lady Ludzenia's military leader, General Faut.

She held her breath as he stepped out from behind the desk. She shuddered with a creepy feeling as he approached. Her heart pounded, her nerves raw, ready to jump if he uttered a sound.

He didn't. He seemed to look her over, his eyes hidden behind dark glasses. He then motioned with his hand at one of the mutant mercenaries before pointing at Thericia.

The mercenary soldier clamped one of its four oversized hands on her shoulder and forced her down to the floor in a corner, against the wall. Pointing its rifle squarely at her, the light from its charge-pak glowing, the mercenary took a step back until it stood against the desk, on guard.

General Faut then waved at the other mercenary and the two of them departed the office without a word.

Now alone in the darkened corner with the mutant aiming its weapon at her head, Thericia broke down and quietly wept. All she wanted was for her father to come fetch her. But she understood what Ludzenia had said, out in the wilderness. There was nothing her father could do to get her out of this predicament. She could only imagine the anguish on her mother's face, especially after their brief talk, earlier in the evening.

Alone, she clasped her hands and lifted her head. "Mother Gheriah," she whimpered, tears rolling down her cheek, "I am so stupid...and sorry for what I've done. Is there any way I can be spared? Can you help? Please?"

She waited in silence without any idea of how much time had passed. Minutes? Hours? She caught a glimpse of a black security eye, a small rounded dome sitting in the ceiling. No doubt, if there was a monitor in the General's office, there would be monitors throughout the ship.

There was no answer to her prayer. There was no hope. Thericia had never felt so lonely in her life, as if she had been mired in a silent, endless void between the many dimensions of the multiverse.

The mutant soldier stood before her, its body unmoving like a statue, its oversized insect-like eyes barely blinking. The leather wings silently folded and unfolded, the scaly tail raised and lowered in the air. Thericia lifted her head and stared at it, wondering what might be in the mind of a laboratory creation. It looked like a grotesque hybrid, a reptiloid body and head with insectoid facial features. Did it get hungry? With the long, calm wait, her stomach had finally settled down and now she was hungry. Was it really motivated only by payment, or did it have feelings like a natural-born being? Did it ever feel fear for its safety, as she now felt?

Thericia took a deep breath and summoned her courage to venture a question. "Do you have a name?"

The mutant soldier did not move.

At least it didn't act threateningly, Thericia told herself. She tried again, this time using the rudimentary Gearmlian tongue she had learned from her language tutor. "Do you have a name?"

This time, it took a step toward her. It opened its jaw and she saw multiple rows of tiny, sharpened incisors within. "Rheerah." Its harsh voice had a distinct, echo-like vibrato and it rolled its consonants as if its tongue was interfering with its speech.

"Rheerah?" Thericia asked, not sure if that was its name.

It was willing to communicate with her. Thericia's mind raced with thoughts of how this could help her situation. It looked monstrous, but could she, in fact, reason with it?

"Rheerah," she said, taking a deep breath, "are you truly a freelance soldier? Are you free to work for anybody?" She waited with taut nerves while it looked her over.

"*Vroomin* are not part of the regular army," it said. "We are free to move about the many worlds of the confederation."

"What about outside the confederation?" she asked.

"We do not leave Gearmlian space."

"You've already left Gearmlian space," she reminded it. "You're on Alscrasian soil. Would you ever work for us, for the right price?" *Would it be willing to work for me?*

It stared at her and blinked, the barrel of its rifle starting to sag downward.

She pressed further. "Are you happy, working for the Gearmlians?"

"I was created for one purpose."

"But life is more than just a job—at least for humans, it has to be. However you came into being, the universe is open to you." Could she possibly work this line of thought to her advantage? She noticed that it was tilting the rifle lower and lower. "You can have more than just that one purpose for existence. You could be more than just a one-dimensional being." Could it think beyond its limitations? "Are you happy, working for the Gearmlians?"

"My allegiance is to the confederation."

"But who is the confederation?" Thericia's

quick blurt surprised even herself. "Who will be the next *Primus*?"

"It is for the College of Electors to decide. For now, Lady Ludzenia is the interim *Primai*."

"But—" Thericia's leaned forward from her sitting position. "Can't you see that life under the deputy *Primai*'s rule could change into one dominated by oppression? You could easily lose your freedom of movement, your freedom of choice. Your only hope for continuity, to keep the way of life you have now, is to promote the King's son."

It turned its head. Left. Right. Up toward the security eye. "The Prince has been arrested."

"What?" Shocked, Thericia felt her breath get knocked out of her. She struggled for a moment to recompose herself. "Why?"

"He is the prime suspect in the King's death."

"That can't be!" Her arms tensed against the confinement of the cuffs. "The Prince loved his father; he would never contemplate something so terrible. It's a lie!"

"It is the truth. He is the only suspect."

"Where is he?" Now her mind was focused. She had known Ludzenia couldn't be trusted, but now she realized how far the woman would go to seize power. "You have to believe me—I was with the Prince when the King passed away. He was heartbroken. Do you know what it's like to lose someone you love?"

She struggled to get to her feet, and the mutant

soldier immediately tensed, cocking the firing mechanism of its rifle and pointing it at her.

"The deputy *Primai* is aiming to take over the confederation," she said. "You can see what her conduct is like."

It seemed to hesitate. The rifle barrel started to waver, again.

"Help me defend the Prince," Thericia pleaded. "Work to change the confederation's course, for your own interests, if not for mine."

A long moment of silence passed. Then, it spoke, softer than before. "He is being held in the storage compartments below the engine room. He is being softened up for interrogation."

Thericia closed her eyes, images of Jomin being held and beaten bloody by monstrous mutant soldiers such as this one filling her heart with despair. He had suffered so much, earlier that evening, watching his father die and struggling with the implication of the post-mortem report.

Priestess Epi's voice suddenly spoke to her. *He must show himself a worthy leader, lonely as it is.* Thericia raged against the words. It didn't have to mean the sort of emotional and physical battering he was undergoing now, did it?

"Please, Rheerah." She took a step toward it. "At least stop the beating. Can you bring him here, under confinement like me?"

"I am not to leave you unguarded."

"Then take me someplace where someone else

can guard me." Thericia stopped again, stunned a second time that she had uttered such powerful words like a command. Could she possibly talk her way out of this room? A new level of understanding seemed to descend upon her. Was this what people like her father did—make changes affecting people with just their words? "I promise not to try anything stupid, if you move me."

Rheerah returned to being statue-like, and as Thericia waited, her patience quickly waned. She could feel her adrenaline race with hope that it might be seriously considering her request. But a quiet, contrary voice kept whispering to her that it had tuned her out and returned to focused guard duty. She needed an answer.

"Rheerah...?"

"I am not interested in being a martyr."

Thericia couldn't believe what she had heard. "I'm not asking you to be a martyr!" She let out a loud groan; her hands fell into her lap with a loud clank of the cuffs. "I'm just asking you to help, not sacrifice yourself." If it wasn't armed with a charge-pak rifle and covered in metal alloy armor, she would have tried to knock some sense into its big-eyed head with her handcuffs.

Rheerah pivoted its head slowly from side to side. "I am sorry."

Sorry! Thericia paused, unsure if it was capable of such feelings or simply saying the words. It was...sorry? For what? Without warning, her rage drained away, leaving her deflated on the floor, and defeated.

With one last ounce of defiance, she muttered, "I'm sorry for your pitiful existence."

5. On the Brink

The lock snapped, the door opened, the light blinded her for a moment.

"Come with us." The two human Gearmlian soldiers had returned. This time, their rifles hung from their belts. No doubt, they knew that they had nothing to guard against. Certainly, not from a young girl.

She obediently rose to her feet, walked past Rheerah with one last bitter look into its oversized eyes, and followed the two down the darkened hallway. Surprisingly, they passed Ludzenia's office and continued through a perpendicular corridor until they reached what looked like the control room of the transport. Monitor screens and computer graphic displays lined the walls. Nearly a dozen uniformed men and woman crowded around the red-lit control stations while a supervisor in a gray cap and trim-fitting uniform hovered over them, giving an occasional order. Standing next to the largest monitor were Lady Ludzenia, General Faut...and between two Gearmlian guards, a hunched-over Prince Jomin in handcuffs.

"Oh my God," Thericia whispered, shocked at the sight of the disheveled Prince.

His scalp was bloodied, and he was bathed in sweat. He had a swollen black eye, surrounded by dark streaks of dried blood that dripped down from his forehead to his neck, a broken nose, and bloodied lips. His shirt was torn open across his chest, a large angry red welt showing itself under the tear. Jomin looked at her with a pensive expression in his hollow eyes. She could only imagine the pain of the beating he had suffered.

Was there anything either of them could do now? For all they knew, Ludzenia could cancel the talks with Alscras, give the order to lift off, and they would be shipped away to the faraway Gearmlian confederation. Thoughts of the rumored asteroid prisons on the far side of confederation space, bordering the Outer Territories, ran through her head. Thericia shut her eyes to try to block out the memories of the Gearmlian mutant soldiers.

"Welcome, young Princess."

Thericia opened her eyes. Ludzenia, exhibiting a vicious smile, now stood in front of her. Thericia averted her eyes from the vile woman and glanced back at Jomin. He was beaten, bruised, and bloodied beyond what she had imagined. His prison escorts remained on either side, cold and on guard. Clearly, he had been "softened," as Rheerah had said. Had he put up a strong resistance against Ludzenia? Had he tried to escape, failed, and been subject to the roughing up?

"I am so glad you are with us," Ludzenia snickered. "The Prince has proved very stubborn and uncooperative."

"Good for him!" Thericia shot out.

Ludzenia shook her head. "We do not need this affair to be dragged out in the courts." After nodding to a technician at a control station to flip a switch, she turned to face the Prince. "I ask you again—do you confess that, by slipping a drug toxic to him without his knowledge, you killed the late King of Breame?"

Jomin, a defiant glare in his eyes now, steadied his posture. He took in a deep breath and spit out, "Go to hell."

Ludzenia sighed. "Our confederation needs reform from the complacency and stagnation of the late King's tenure. There is so much work to be done. A confession would spare all our people from having to endure an extended period of mourning."

"Then confess!" Thericia directed her words not at Jomin, but at Ludzenia. "You're trying to frame the Prince for a killing which you, yourself, ordered. Tell everyone that you want to seize control of the confederation."

General Faut stepped over. "That is a baseless

accusation."

"No, it's not." Thericia locked eyes with the now-silent Ludzenia. The Princess knew that both women understood what she had meant.

The recorder was on. Thericia could describe what she had seen the deputy *Primai* doing in the hills. Would it sound like the wild ramblings of a fanciful young girl, or could she possibly threaten Ludzenia's stature with a rational, plausible statement of the bizarre?

"Let us go, unharmed," Thericia said, "and I will let this incident drop." It was a lie, of course, but it was her only strategy.

Ludzenia tilted her head. "Perhaps I should think this over." She returned her gaze to the Prince.

"Let her go," Jomin growled.

Ludzenia shook her head. "Perhaps the Prince should consider the potential ramifications...to the Princess."

Thericia gasped.

Ludzenia let out a sly smile. "I am truly glad that you are here to help the Prince come to his senses."

"No," Thericia muttered with a sinking feeling in her stomach. By her own actions, she had fallen into the clutches of Lady Ludzenia and was now a useful pawn in the deputy *Primai*'s designs against the Prince.

General Faut waved his black gloved hand and half a dozen mutant mercenaries stepped out of the shadows between the various control stations. All had their rifles aimed squarely at Thericia, their charge-paks pulsating—including, Thericia recognized, Rheerah.

She struggled to stifle a whimper, but a mortal fear enveloped her. Thericia didn't want to die, not now, not here, not at the hands of these beings.

"Leave her alone!" Jomin yelled at Ludzenia.

The deputy *Primai* glanced up at a speaker in the ceiling. The recorder wad still on. "Do you confess, Your Highness? You can spare our people— and the young Princess—with a simple statement of the truth."

Jomin paused. Thericia stared at the Prince with uncertainty, her breath held, her heart pounding, her head teetering toward vertigo. He balanced both her life and the fate of the confederation in his hands.

The captain of the ship abruptly rose from the monitor, breaking Thericia's attention. "Something's happening outside."

Thericia whipped her head over. She could see most of the image on the monitor from where they stood. It was an exterior view of the outside of the transport. It was light, perhaps daybreak, and the terminal building stood several dozen yards away. Multiple platoons of Alscrasian soldiers were lined up near the terminal, at attention, with their rifles drawn. About a dozen vehicles were moving into position behind the foot soldiers. The obvious thought—and hope—was that the army had arrived to liberate her. Her pulse quickened with anticipation. Would Ludzenia release her immediately, or after a protracted negotiation?

Ludzenia stepped over to face Thericia. "It seems we have a 'situation' developing." She smiled. "Captain, place the ship at battle stations."

Thericia tensed.

"All hands to battle stations," the captain ordered.

She hadn't expected Ludzenia to open fire like a madwoman. The Gearmlian transport was just a single visiting ship, sitting in the middle of the Alscrasian star base. It couldn't possibly survive a fight. Was Ludzenia only bluffing?

The klaxon sounded as several additional control stations came to life. Displays switched to tactical charts and calculations. On the rear display, a power plant energy diagram began counting up. "Bridge to all stations," the captain ordered, "energize weapons."

"What are you doing?" Jomin shouted. "We are not at war!"

More armed soldiers entered the control room, assuming positions between each of the stations with rifles and *cuxioblades* hanging from their belts. Alarmed, Thericia looked back at the exterior monitor. Two armored gun platforms had moved into position, flanking the troops on either side. On a second monitor along the far wall, a similar lineup was forming on the other side of the transport. Thericia hoped that they wouldn't open fire on them, but if Ludzenia shot first, the Alscrasian forces would have to answer.

Jomin struggled against his guards, unable to approach Ludzenia, General Faut, or the captain. "I order you to stand down."

Regardless of how the situation was quickly changing, Thericia didn't want to die. She looked at Jomin, who remained focused on Ludzenia through all the activity. The situation felt hopeless, and she whispered a prayer to Mother Gheriah, asking for a divine intervention.

"Transmission coming in," said the comm officer.

Ludzenia nodded.

Faut ordered, "Put it on the speaker."

A crackle of static sounded. "Deputy *Primai* Ludzenia." Thericia jumped at the sound of her father's voice. "We demand the immediate release of the Princess of Alscras."

Thericia held her breath as Ludzenia pointed her finger at the comm officer to broadcast.

"Your Majesty," the deputy *Primai* said in a measured, diplomatic tone, "as I stated in my report, the Princess was captured having violated the terms of the Bexelian Agreement. Gearmlian sovereignty is paramount to the confederation, even under imperial membership, and espionage is a serious capital offense. She must be held accountable in a court of law and tried under the terms of the Agreement, in a special tribunal according to Gearmlian custom. Surely, you must agree that upholding the laws of our empire is our most important duty."

Thericia squeezed her hands together in a vain attempt to calm her trembling body. It never occurred to her that she might have been spying on the deputy *Primai*. She only knew that Ludzenia held a dangerous secret plan, which she had to communicate to her father.

"Deputy *Primai* Ludzenia." It was her father, again. "We do not disagree regarding the terms of the Bexelian Agreement and we respect confederation sovereignty. Nor do we disagree regarding the Princess' offense." Thericia's stomach dropped. With her father's words, the full gravity of her situation fell squarely upon her. "The Princess will be held accountable, but by imperial oversight and under Alscrasian law. Turn her over to us, and we will deal with her offense."

Ludzenia howled with laughter. Faut gave her a knowing smile.

"Your Majesty," Ludzenia said, "we have the deeper question of the Princess's role in the assassination of the *Primus*. We had assumed that it was strictly an internal affair, but it appears we are mistaken." She eyed Thericia. "The Princess may be in league with Prince Jomin to elevate him to the chair of the confederation."

Thericia couldn't hold it any longer. She charged toward the speaker. "It's a lie! She's the one scheming to take over—"

"Hold her!" General Faut ordered, as two Gearmlian soldiers pulled Thericia away.

"Let her go!" Jomin yelled. Two more soldiers immediately restrained him. When he fought back, one of the soldiers punched him in the stomach. "Argh!" Jomin doubled over in pain and collapsed to the floor.

"No!" Thericia screamed.

"Let me talk to her," the Emperor demanded over the speaker.

"All in good order, Your Majesty," Ludzenia said in a calm, restrained tone, hushing all the commotion. After Jomin was pulled back up to his feet, Ludzenia continued. "We have much to sort through, so you will forgive us if we wait for an available opportunity for you to communicate with Her Highness."

"I'm right here!" Thericia yelled.

Ludzenia whipped her arm through the air, her pointy-nailed index finger mere inches away from Thericia's face, silencing the Princess. After staring at Thericia for a long mo-ment, she said, "All right." With slow, measured syllables, the deputy *Primai* said, "Perhaps the young Princess should explain why she followed me and spied on me."

Thericia didn't know what to say. The words "to help the Prince" would have fallen right into Ludzenia's accusation. She didn't dare glance at Jomin, either. Thericia could only stare at the floor, her mind a jumble.

"Your Majesty," Ludzenia said, "can you elicit the truth from her?"

"Thericia?" The quaver in her father's voice broke Thericia's heart. With military forces lined up to face off, she struggled with the realization that she had put him in this position. "Are you all right?"

Thericia took a deep breath to steady herself. She cleared her throat. "I'm all right."

"What happened?"

She could feel all eyes—Lady Ludzenia's, General Faut's, the Gearmlian military personnel surrounding them, Prince Jomin's, and even her father's from wherever he was positioned—weighing down on her. This was her chance to state her accusation. But she knew now that she couldn't go off about what she saw in the hills. With Ludzenia's new accusation against Thericia, no one would believe her wild descriptions about the Wa'ohl'thu. She also knew that she had no evidence supporting her belief in Jomin's innocence, just her intuition.

"Thericia?"

"I'm sorry, Your Majesty," Ludzenia said. "We cannot overlook the possibility that the young Princess was somehow aiding our primary suspect, the Prince of Breame."

"That's a false accusation!" Jomin yelled toward the speaker.

"We must investigate the matter for ourselves."

Ludzenia smiled at Thericia, a malicious leer from the depths of a heart of darkness. "We will keep the Princess safe, in solitary confinement."

"No...." Thericia gasped. Her arms and legs tensed and she felt the constricting tug of the two soldiers restraining her movement. She wanted to lunge for the deputy *Primai*'s neck and twist it with her bare hands.

"You will do no such thing," the Emperor said. "We will take the Princess into custody, and she will be subject to imperial justice."

Thericia caught a momentary squint in Ludzenia's eye. It was only an instant as the deputy *Primai* seemed to scowl at the image of the Alscrasian troops on the monitor. But for Thericia, it brought back the undeniable demonic feelings she felt as she watched Ludzenia during the night. The woman may have looked human, seemed human, been human, but there was something deeply inhuman about her. Thericia could feel it in her bones. She looked at Jomin, his face covered in sweat from the pain of the blow, and tried to picture what further torture he could undergo in the secret Gearmlian prisons at the hands of the mutant soldiers.

Ludzenia turned to General Faut. "We are at an end. Prepare for departure."

"With pleasure." Faut turned to the transport captain. "Bring the thrusters online. Target all weapons."

"You're insane!" Jomin charged.

Thericia sensed a subtle hum in the walls and floor. A low rumble became discernible in her ears. The whirl and loud clicks of heavy machinery echoed all about them. The weapons systems, Thericia realized, guns moving into position. Some, no doubt, were aimed at the terminal building. Then Thericia tensed. This was a space vehicle—and the weapons could potentially reach farther than just the buildings of the star base. Could they fire upon the city? Upon the capital? The State Building? The palace?

"Deputy *Primai* Ludzenia," the Emperor's voice boomed, "disarm your weapons, immediately."

On the monitor, the Alscrasian troops took up forward positions surrounding the transport.

"Would you give the order to open fire upon a sovereign vessel of the empire, Your Majesty?" Ludzenia asked with a sneer.

"I will wage war to prevent my daughter's abduction."

Thericia felt an overwhelming protective love in her father's words. She knew that her father was a man of his word. If he said he would go to war for her, he would, coldly, rationally employing the best military strategists, and issuing orders to the most powerful star fleet in Eurania. At the same time, it sank in that he commanded military firepower beyond her comprehension. She had never feared him before. As a small child facing her father's punishment, yes, but not the sense of awe that she felt now. The contradicting emotions conflicted her as she listened to her father's voice.

"Our satellites have targeted your vessel." The Emperor's voice boomed over the speaker. "If you harm the Princess, we will destroy you and all aboard. Release her, immediately!"

"Weapons ready," the weapons officer reported.

"No!" It was Jomin, pulling himself against the Gearmlian guards. "I order this ship to stand down."

"Do you all want to die?" Thericia screamed at the crew.

Ludzenia turned to Faut. "Let the fun begin."

Thericia held her breath, bracing herself for the imminent explosions, and her end. From the corner of her eye, she saw Rheerah reach toward the control console.

Just then, the main security monitor flickered and its image abruptly changed. A sharp voice said, "Leave me!" Thericia saw a recording of a woman —Lady Ludzenia—ordering a pair of mercenary soldiers out of an empty room.

"What's that?" Ludzenia spun, her robe and hair a wild, whirling blur.

A security guard suddenly swung the butt of his charge-pak rifle, belting Rheerah across the side of its oversized head. Thericia screamed as four security guards tackled the screaming, struggling Rheerah, crushing it under their combined weight and pinning its many arms down to the floor. A fifth guard leveled his firearm at Rheerah's head.

"Don't hurt him!" Thericia yelled in realization that the mercenary had turned. A streak of blood ran across Rheerah's forehead from the hit.

"Turn that off!" Ludzenia ordered.

But it was too late. Thericia saw footage of Ludzenia replacing a small bottle on a counter in the empty room with an identical container from her pocket before a crewman switched off the monitor.

"You!" Jomin hissed, his eyes fierce.

Thericia—and everybody—now knew that it had to be the King's medication and the Cepiadrine, switched by Lady Ludzenia, herself.

"You traitor!" Jomin yelled as he pulled against his guards, sweat pouring down his body.

The squint in the deputy *Primai*'s eyes, the ugly twist on her blood-red lips, the look of death she sent Jomin's direction, shot a chill down Thericia's spine. The woman raged within, ready to kill.

"Deputy *Primai* Ludzenia."

All eyes turned to face the speaker that the Emperor's voice came through.

"We have received your transmission."

A surge of triumphant hope rushed through Thericia. Her father had captured the smoking gun on the deputy *Primai*.

"No!" Ludzenia snarled. "The footage is fake." She jabbed a finger at the speaker. "A fake, I tell you!"

"I will consider your argument," the Emperor

said in a calm voice, "if you release the Princess. Immediately."

Thericia saw Ludzenia huff several times before her shoulders finally slumped. The deputy *Primai* had been caught, with no way out besides the one option offered by the Emperor.

Ludzenia whirled around to face Thericia. "Stupid girl!"

Thericia steeled her nerves. "Release the Prince, too."

Ludzenia turned back to the speaker. "How do I know you won't double-cross me?" she roared.

"I am your Emperor," the voice boomed. "My word is my bond."

A silence filled the control room. The Emperor had spoken. Imperial honor, something Thericia's tutors had alluded to many times during her education, was now before her. She realized it was the unique, special quality that separated her father from someone like Ludzenia. It was also something that was paramount to Thericia's standing as the Princess, and to her future.

"Stand down your weapons," the Emperor ordered, "and release the Princess. To show good faith, we will pull back our troops."

Thericia watched as the forward Alscrasian soldiers slowly backed away from the transport. Their rifles were still aimed at the enemy, but with each step, the tension decreased.

She turned her gaze back to deputy *Primai*

Ludzenia, in anticipation of the next move. She could tell that Ludzenia struggled with the decision. If Ludzenia took the Emperor's offer, she would remain a contender for the leadership of the confederation—and so would her primary adversary, Prince Jomin, who would escape from her foul clutches.

"Release the Princess," Ludzenia bellowed to Faut. After a short pause, she spit out, "The Prince, as well." She motioned to the technician to turn off the speaker.

"Very well," Faut grumbled. Pointing at Rheerah, he said, "Take him away." He waved his hand at the guards and they pulled the bloodied, struggling Rheerah to his feet.

"No!" Thericia called out. More than anyone else, she owed her life to the strange laboratory creation. "He comes with us."

"You are in no position to issue orders to the deputy *Primai*," Faut said.

Ludzenia remained silent as Thericia took a step toward her. It was a titanic roll of the dice that the young Princess could never have imagined.

"If he stays, I stay," Thericia said, struggling to keep her fear in check, "and you will have no bargain with the Emperor."

Ludzenia stared her at Thericia, took a step away to stand next to General Faut, gave Thericia a second hard look with her piercing black eyes, and with lightning speed, took Faut's pistol from his belt and blasted Rheerah in a bloody explosion that showered over everyone.

Thericia screamed as blood splattered over her. She collapsed to her knees, overwhelmed with grief at Rheerah's execution.

"You witch!" Thericia lost her composure, threw her hands over her face, and wailed openly.

She didn't understand what she had gotten herself into. The memories of Wa'ohl'thu burned in Thericia's mind. Ludzenia had supplicated the Keeper of Souls, somehow summoning it to appear before her. Who exactly was this horrid woman, and what would be the ramification of leaving her in power?

"Silence!" Ludzenia ordered. She eyed Thericia, still quietly sobbing. Handing the pistol back to Faut, the blood-drenched Ludzenia said, "You may leave, Your Highnesses."

The Prince, released from his guards, quickly stepped over to Thericia, put his arm around her shoulders, and said, "We need to go." Shooting Ludzenia a cold stare, he added, "You need to leave this planet."

Now, Thericia understood that there could be no clear triumph today, only a step away from a heightened state of crisis. The peace of the empire was the long term priority. So was Thericia's sur-vival. Try as she might, she couldn't stifle her emotions. She was too small, and the complexities of the crisis were too overwhelming.

Ludzenia gave Thericia an evil stare. "General," she spit out, "get her out of my sight."

Torrence had somehow found his way home, without harm, back to his stable, and the imperial physician had confirmed that Thericia had not been injured. But, she was miserable. Upon her safe return to the palace, each of her attendants, without exception, came before the Princess to express their relief at her release from captivity and to offer whatever help she might desire from them. Each had been dismissed, leaving her alone in her room. Young or old, innocent or experienced, Thericia couldn't find it in herself to share her feelings with any of them.

She had befriended the Prince, had felt his pain and his loss, had tried to comfort him. She had risked her life to help him.

Without warning, a soft voice spoke in her head. *"The Prince must show himself a worthy leader, lonely as it is. It is, in fact, a reality you may need to face...."*

"Stop it!" she cried, diving into her bed and covering her head with a pillow. "Please stop."

Priestess Epi's voice didn't stop, but as the words repeated, they slowly faded like a dying echo. After a few minutes, her head stopped hurting. She threw the pillow aside and turned over to stare at the ceiling. An electro-painting of a light blue sky full of white, fluffy clouds drifted by, soothing her nerves and clearing her head.

A lot had happened in a very short time. Her dance with Prince Jomin and her surprising feelings for him. The King's sudden death during the state dinner. Her meeting with Lady Ludzenia. Her visit with Priestess Epi. Prince Jomin's arrest. The mysterious Wa'ohl'thu's secret appearance. Her talk with Rheerah. The near-outbreak of war.

In the end, she had not helped Jomin, not really. He had not helped himself, either. They had both been over their head in their confrontation with the deputy *Primai*. It had been her father who came to their rescue. Her father and Rheerah.

She had won the mutant's loyalty, and he paid for his decision in a brutal, savage, inhuman killing.

"Why?" She turned back over and re-buried her head in her pillow. "Please let it all be a bad dream."

In her heart, Thericia finally understood that Priestess Epi had been right. Her attraction to Prince Jomin had dictated her decisions. That was where everything became confusing, where she got herself into trouble. It had cost Rheerah his life.

She knew she had to face her father. She owed him her life. She also owed him an explanation for how she had brought the empire to near disaster. Even now, she didn't know for sure how things had deteriorated so rapidly from a festive banquet to a military face-off in just a single night. Somehow, she had to convince her father of the true nature of deputy *Primai* Ludzenia. Everything that had transpired was because of that secret. Otherwise, she might be subject to imperial incarceration—something that was unheard of, but not impossible.

Thericia rose out of bed, shook her head to try to clear it, and without further thought, departed her room for the long trek to her parents' room. She passed one door after another, stopped at the landing to glance down the grand staircase at the foyer and the oversized front door, then continued on. There was nothing to be gained by delaying further.

She reached her parents' room and was about to knock when the sound of her father's voice, booming through the door, gave her pause.

"What are we going to do with her?"

"Otias, lower your voice!" It was her mother, now. "People will hear."

Thericia pressed her ear against the door. Her mother's voice lowered, but was still discernible.

"I'm sure she didn't mean to do anything dangerous."

"Didn't she? Going out in the middle of the night to spy on the deputy *Primai*?" Her father was still livid. "Why didn't you stop her?"

"I tried, but she's headstrong."

"That's no excuse. She knows better, and you shouldn't have been so lenient."

"Otias, she's in love, her first."

"Jarina, she almost took us to war—"

Thericia pulled away from the door. She had never heard her parents arguing so heatedly. The words hurt. What her father said was true. She didn't know how to make amends to him. Troubled and heartbroken, she started back for her room with tears in her eyes.

When she reached the landing overlooking the stairs, she stopped. The grand majesty of the wide circular steps made an impression upon her. She was still the Alscrasian Princess. Inadvertent or not, she could wield great power that affected—or could change—the lives of others.

She couldn't cower in her room.

Reluctant, but with what little resolve she could muster, she returned to her parents' door. She couldn't hear the voices, any longer. The discussion, apparently, had ended. She took a deep breath, knocked, and waited.

The door opened and her father peered out. "Thericia?"

Thericia nodded.

His face relaxed a touch and he swung the door open. "Come in."

Thericia followed him inside. Her mother, who was sitting in her usual chair, writing on her porta-com, smiled and gestured for Thericia to sit in the chair opposite hers. It was Thericia's customary spot, whenever she visited her mother, and she immediately headed for the comfort of the familiar. But when she reached it, she paused, her mind still focused on her task. She could not sit until she had addressed what she needed to address.

She turned to face her father, the Emperor. "Father." Her voice was barely audible. She knew she had to speak clearly and cleanly, as becoming of a member of the royal family. She lowered her eyes. "Father, I owe you an apology for my conduct." Her voice cracked. "I showed very poor judgment in my actions." She struggled to keep from breaking down in tears, but despite the tremble in her voice, she continued on. "I am ready for whatever discipline is due me, whether it be yours or the state's."

Her father's imposing figure towered before her. A pair of large, firm hands held her shoulders. She looked up into his face and saw his eyes glistening. His voice was strong and commanding. "What were you thinking, child?"

Thericia could only lower her head. "I wasn't. Priestess Epi said I was being led by my feelings for the Prince. She was right. My conduct was not worthy of a Princess of Alscras."

A long silence imposed itself between them.

Thericia took a deep breath and asked, "What's going to happen to me?"

The Emperor cleared his throat. "I will discuss the appropriate measures with Mr. Franklen." A sigh. "You're in very serious trouble, Thericia."

"Yes, Father." That was all she could say. The answer confirmed the worst of her fears. She had no idea what "the appropriate measures" meant. More than a paddling, but...prison? Could it be possible that her father didn't know, either?

"You're sixteen," her father continued. "You're second in line to the throne of Alscras, yet you know so little about the world in which you live, and in which I work."

"How could I?" Thericia blurted out on impulse, her flailing arms swatting his hands away. "I know nothing but gowns and dinners and dances, and every time I start to ask, I come away feeling that it's not for me to know anything—"

She stopped herself, but she couldn't take back what had already come out. "I'm sorry, but that's how I feel." She looked up at him, feeling very small and powerless before her Emperor. He stood tall over her, but his eyes were soft.

"Please sit."

Thericia obeyed, taking the chair that she had held off sitting in. Her father then reached over, took hold of a chair, and set it before her. Seating himself, he glanced at Jarina before clearing his voice, again. When he opened his mouth and hesitated, lowering his head into his hand, she held her breath, unsure of what was coming.

With a loud inhale, he raised his head, his eyebrows furled. "Thericia..." He let out another sigh. "You are correct. I have put all my attention to preparing your brother for public life, and to someday succeed me. I have completely overlooked you. For that, I apologize."

Thericia wasn't sure she heard correctly. She had never seen her father vulnerable before. He was her King and her Emperor, the first among the powerful. Now, he spoke as her father. The words touched her heart and she now saw him differently. He was a man like any other man, one who tried to do the best he could with what he had, but who came up short to those closest to him.

"You truly are a capable young woman, fearless, and full of compassion. You have the power to put your thoughts into action with swift decisiveness. It is clear that you are every bit as able as your brother. You only lack the education and training that I have been providing him."

She had hoped to hear these words from him many times, especially after an official function when she had to say a few words as a member of the royal family, or perform a riding exhibition on Torrence. He would usually give her a brief compliment, sometimes with a warm hug, but he never elaborated on her as either the Princess or his daughter, not even in private. As the years passed, Thericia concluded that it was simply not his style and ceased hoping for it. Instead, she had turned to the privacy of her journal, and it had become a warm, comfortable retreat.

"When this whole affair has blown over, you should begin learning about the empire. Not just the academic subject matter, but all of it. As my aide."

Thericia gasped. As the Emperor's aide?

Her father took a deep breath and as he continued, his voice became gentler and less commanding. "It will be a lot of work. The empire is a vast and dynamic entity, ever growing, ever changing, but you will see and touch it as it unfolds before you. Do you agree?"

Thericia hesitated. "I...don't know what to say." It was true, she didn't know. She finally had her opportunity, something she had privately grumbled about numerous times over the years, and yet, the offer before her felt as overwhelming as the events of the past day.

Her father chuckled to break the tension. "I suggest you say, 'yes.' You managed to single-handedly bring the empire to the brink of war. As your father, I strongly advise you to learn how to conduct yourself in the larger world, for your own sake, and for the wellbeing of the empire."

It made sense. Her father's words usually did. It was just that the larger world felt, well, large. Very large. Thericia looked to her mother, who gave her a nod and a smile. With a deep, determined breath, Thericia said, "Yes."

Her father leaned forward, and this time, the hug felt different. Special. Close. Thericia didn't want the embrace to end.

A knock on the door sounded, interrupting the moment, to Thericia's disappointment. The Emperor released her, rose from his chair, and walked to the door.

"Excuse me, Your Majesty," an aide said. "There is a visitor for the Princess."

Thericia stood up, curious. "Who?"

"The Prince of Breame. He came alone."

Thericia glanced at her father, and at her mother, who was still seated, then told the aide, "I'll come down."

After the aide departed, the Emperor's face changed back to a serious, somber expression. "I'll go see what Mr. Franklen can do on your behalf."

Thericia followed her father out of the room. While he headed down the side stairs to the offices, Thericia rounded the corner, reaching the overlook at the top of the grand staircase. From there, she saw Prince Jomin, alone in the entry foyer.

He had changed to a clean uniform, but Jomin's head was bandaged all over—across his forehead, over his nose, his lips. His black eye seemed larger and darker than before.

Thericia's heart ached at the sight as she walked down the staircase. Without warning, the memories of his beaten appearance rushed into her mind and she charged down the stairs. When she reached the bottom, she ran across the foyer to Jomin, happy to see him, but concerned for his condition.

She didn't know whether to give him a hug or not. "Jomin, I'm so glad to see you."

Without another thought, she embraced him— and he jerked back with a muffled grimace.

"I'm so sorry!" she said, remembering the bright

red welt across his chest. She couldn't believe she had so carelessly forgotten.

"It's...okay," he managed to say between coughs. With several deep breaths, he recomposed himself, straightening his stance. "I wanted to come see how you were doing."

"I'm all right," she said, touched that he was concerned about her. "Did the doctor examine your injuries?"

"It'll take a few weeks, but I'll be fine."

He reached out and took her hands. Despite his injuries, the feeling of his touch hadn't changed from the night of the state dinner, on the dance floor. His grip was still as warm and as comforting as before, and she could feel her hands start to tremble ever so slightly, again.

"Thericia," he spoke her name softly, "I wanted to thank you for defending me."

She lowered her head. "I wasn't much help."

"On the contrary," Jomin said, "you are one of the most courageous persons I've ever met. Lady Ludzenia is a formidable opponent, and I consider myself lucky to have the support of both you and the Emperor." He drew in his breath. "You're an inspiration to me."

She gazed into his soft, blue eyes as he drew her closer, her mind lost in the moment. She opened her mouth to say something, but no words came out. She knew what was coming. He was so close. It felt right, but....

"Uh," she forced out, almost a gasp, "not...now." She gave his hands a tight squeeze as she pushed herself back a step. She wanted badly to kiss his hurt lips, even with the bandage there, but instead, she let his hands go and her eyes teared up. "I'm...sorry." Hearing him sigh, she looked up into his darkened, bruised eyes.

"It's fine," he whispered. "It's just, well,..." The discouragement in his voice obvious. "I just want you with me. I know that now."

He wanted her. She wanted him. This was where she got herself into trouble.

"Maybe...someday...." She faltered.

Jomin stepped closer. "Come with me."

Thericia froze. Had she had heard correctly? "Pardon?"

"I'll be returning to Breame within the week to prepare for the College of Electors," he said. "Come with me—to Breame. I need you."

Thericia was torn, her heart ripping in half. "My father has offered me an opportunity with him."

"Please, dear Princess...." His face exuded pain.

Thericia sadly shook her head. "I can't." She took a deep breath, which didn't help her resolve, and spoke stoically. "For my own good, and for the wellbeing of the empire." She took his hands. "You understand, don't you?"

The Prince of Breame nodded, but the pain of rejection still showed in his eyes. He lifted her hand to his lips and gently kissed it. "I wish you all the best. If you ever change your mind, please re-member that I'll be waiting."

Before she could say another word, he bowed to her, opened the front door, and stepped out.

After he climbed aboard his hover-mobile and departed, Thericia closed the door and rested her head against it, struggling to hold her tears in. How could she hurt him like that?

Her mother stepped out from behind a nearby column and took her hands. "Are you all right, Thericia?"

Thericia didn't know how much her mother had overheard, but she remembered what her mother had said to her after the state dinner. *You're my only daughter. I don't want you to be hurt. Be very, very careful with your feelings for the Prince.* Thericia's confusion threatened to overwhelm her. Her mother's inviting arms opened, offering her comfort, warmth, and a safe retreat.

But then, Thericia remembered the wise words of Priestess Epi. The young Princess had taken her first steps into the sphere of interstellar politics. Now, she had to live out her title as the Princess of an interstellar empire.

With a deep breath, Thericia reached out and gave her mother a firm, heartfelt embrace. "I'll be all right, Mother."

Postlude

Two small, missile-like escort destroyers, their pulse cannons energized and flashing, appeared in the sky. A black transport—an exact replica of the accursed craft that had departed the week before with deputy *Primai* Ludzenia, General Faut, and the body of Rheerah—followed. Finally, the largest vessel of the group, a sleek silver Breamian Star Yacht, descended through the clouds.

Thericia, dressed again as when Prince Jomin first arrived, watched the lumbering transport circle high overhead, the memories of Ludzenia and Faut still fresh on her mind, while the royal Star Yacht hovered toward the middle of the empty pad. She marveled at the fact that the starcraft would be traversing the vast distance across the empire to the confederation in a matter of a couple short weeks, ferrying Jomin back home to Breame.

As she took her place next to her mother and

brother, a few steps behind her father, Thericia thought about the situation in the Gearmlian Confederation. The members of the College of Electors, representatives from all the Gearmlian planets, were already gathering on Gearml-5. Over the next month, they would be choosing the new *Primus*. The rulers of the industrial planet, Kearo, and the military-dominated world, Gassil, had been nominated, along with Lady Ludzenia of Broza and Prince Jomin of Breame. More than ever, she hoped that Jomin would succeed his late father. Unfortunately, the long shadow of Ludzenia cast a dark cloud over those aspirations.

After exchanging farewells with the Emperor, the Queen, and Prince Otias, Jomin approached Thericia. She could see that his bruises were already fading.

"Are you certain you won't accept my offer?" he asked her.

Thericia nodded with a downcast glance. "It's best. I have a lot of work to focus on."

Jomin's offer was tempting, but now was not the time to explore a deeper friendship with the Prince.

"It's been decided that I am to work for the Gearmlian ambassador for a year," Thericia said, her eyes staring at the ground, "partly for my education and partly as restitution."

"I'm sorry for that," Jomin said.

Thericia shrugged her shoulders. "It's the agreement, and a plausible story for the public with no real ramifications. After that, I'll transfer to my father's staff to begin working for him."

She still bristled at the thought of being the lone scapegoat for the incident, while Ludzenia's standing emerged unscathed. With a muffled groan, she tried—unsuccessfully—to dismiss the bitterness. This was how things worked, a lesson she needed to learn if she was to participate successfully in the world of politics. While it might have been in the guise of remittance, she was entering her father's sphere.

"Maybe, someday, you could be the Emperor's liaison," Jomin said, "and we could work together."

"Maybe." She looked up. "I'd like that."

How the election would go, no one knew for certain. The Emperor had told Thericia, in private, that he was banking on Prince Jomin winning, thus ending Lady Ludzenia's ambitions and rendering the consequences of his decision to spare the deputy *Primai* moot. But Thericia knew better, and she had told him so. The woman was a killer. She was also some sort of sorceress. Though Thericia had no tangible evidence to support such a conclusion, she would never forget the memories of the night in the hills of Zemuir.

After the Star Yacht landed, a large underside bay opened, and a decorated military hover-mobile emerged. It floated down the ship's wide ramp onto the causeway and traversed the short stretch to the terminal.

Without warning, her mind flashed back to the nightmare in the transport control room, and she suddenly grasped his arm. "Be very careful."

"I will."

He bent down and gave her a kiss on the forehead. With a sudden, unexpected realization that this might be goodbye, Thericia flung aside any restraints she had over her feelings, threw her arms around Jomin, and kissed him on the lips. To her surprise, he pulled her closer and returned her kiss.

It was a long embrace. Thericia knew that the moment had been captured by the media and would be relayed through the interstellar comm-relays to the empire and beyond. She would become fodder for the vultures of the celebrity gossip circuit.

For right now, she didn't care. She felt his warmth, the softness of his lips, and she didn't want the moment to end. So much had changed in her world since his arrival. Her heart kept close the memory of their brief time together. It had felt magical, it had felt right.

She knew that he was the one.

But with great effort, she let go and stoically watched as he backed away to his sedan. While everyone stood at attention, the band then played the anthem of the confederation, followed by the anthem of the empire.

Slowly, ten imperial soldiers marched out of the terminal, bearing the flag-draped casket of the late *Primus*, King Priot of Breame. Thericia gazed at the coffin in somber silence.

There was one undeniable difference between her and Jomin. Her father was still alive and well, and she was grateful for that. Prince Jomin was alone, all alone.

Her mother placed her hands over Thericia's shoulders as the music ended. "We will all keep faith in his wellbeing."

Thericia glanced at the ring on her finger, the one that she had received from Priestess Epi. The bond between a young woman and her first man was mysterious, indeed. Whether she and the Prince would have occasion to cross paths again, she didn't know, but her intuitive feeling suggested that anything was possible.

The End